The Typing Room

The Typing Room

Monica De Vargas

The New
Atlantian Library

THE NEW ATLANTIAN LIBRARY
is an imprint of
ABSOLUTELY AMAZING eBOOKS

Published by Whiz Bang LLC, 926 Truman Avenue, Key West, Florida 33040, USA.

For information contact:
Publisher@AbsolutelyAmazingEbooks.com
ISBN-13:978-0692438930 (New Atlantian Library, The)
ISBN-10:0692438939

For Stella

"And do not be conformed to this world,
but be transformed by the renewing of your mind…"

~ Romans 12:2

The
Typing
Room

Prologue

The Proprietress was always an excellent storyteller. It would be like you were right there to hear her tell about something. In the style of a medieval raconteur, she would spin an entertaining tale out of the ordinary happenings in the neighborhood, or in her life, or in the lives of those around her at work or at home, and you might feel as if you had just read a good book. It was the same with films. So fine and affecting were her descriptions of the characters and camera work and plot lines it was as if you had seen the movie. And then, sadly, it was, over time, as if the bookstores closed their doors, one by one, and when the reruns had overstayed their welcome, all the screens in all the theatres of her life went dark. So now she needed someone else's stories. But there was no way to get them. Except in The Typing Room.

"What makes you think this will work?" The Newcomer asked. "I don't see how it can. It's really just so much nonsense!"

"You're here, aren't you?" she said, matter-of-factly. "Explain that and then tell me why you have such doubts. Were you always this much of a 'query wart'?"

"I'm sure you mean that in the nicest of ways, but it's not even a real word!" he snapped back. "You can't just make things up."

"Oh, but I can. Be patient, and learn, my friend. Be patient, and learn."

"Why would they do it? It's just crazy to expect them to come at all, much less do what you are asking them to do."

"Be that as it may, but come they do, and have for a long time now." She shifted her focus to the others. "Shall I begin?"

"Oh, yes. Please," they said, almost in unison.

"Very well," she said in a studied way. "'My name is Corrine, and I've been here before. I hope you remember me, so that I don't have to explain too much about why I am here now..."

And they all nodded with satisfaction because they did remember her. Very well, in fact.

Chapter I

She was late. Late with the rent, late for work, and now, as she stood in front of the calendar on the back of the bathroom door, late for the one thing which could truly be called a curse. If only she'd been awake when he came home this last time. If only he hadn't smelled so good, and felt so warm, as he climbed into bed with her, being particularly quiet so as to not wake the two little girls sleeping just a few feet away in the roll-away bed behind a makeshift screen in their one-room flat. They made love slowly as he entered her from behind, lying together like two spoons in a drawer. He liked it that way, and so did she. He held her close and buried his face in her hair and in her neck, all the while saying things to her only a husband would dare to say. When she woke up it was as if she had been dreaming, but she could still smell him and felt the slippery silk he left behind. And this morning she found the note. *"Dearest Petunia, I've got to leave. Times are hard, and there's no work for a man like me here. I'll write when I can. Kiss the girls for me. Your loving husband, Rusty Storm."* So she was alone and late, and the girls were beginning to stir, and faces would need to be washed and teeth brushed and hair braided. Then six-year-old Doris, who seemed far too old and wise beyond reason, asked for her Daddy, and seeing her mother's woeful expression, smirked as she took charge of her younger sister, Aimee. Now Corrine wasn't sure about a lot of things, but she was certain of one. It was time to visit The Typing Room.

It was not really like selling your soul. You were just pawning it, a little at a time. She went there once before, when Rusty had been gone for two months. There was no food and the girls needed to visit the doctor, and she felt too proud and too angry to go to the county hospital and stand in line with the other charity cases. So it seemed like an answered prayer when she saw the little ad tucked away at the back of the paper between the Want Ads and the Personals.

> *"Need Help? Bills due? Tired of ducking the Landlord? Come One...Come All to The Typing Room! We pay good, honest Money for your Story of Desperation and Despair."*

And then the address, which turned out to be a small room at the top of a four-story walk-up, at the end of a quiet residential street, in a faded but still fashionable area of the city.

The singular room was as she remembered it. Pleasant and bright, not at all what she had imagined given the strange nature of the ad. The rug was an antique, slightly worn, in deep shades of burgundy and blue, but the wall covering was a smooth buttery fabric which she now realized might be chamois, wrapped around some sort of padding, giving the room a womb-like quality. There was one tall curtainless window with ornate framing and molding which looked out onto the street and over to a small triangular-shaped park. Near the window, on the left side of a sleek, black desk, was a tailored shaded lamp, and a neat stack of heavy crème colored typing bond, a pencil cup with one #2 Ticonderoga pencil and a small brass well with a quill pen dipped in the black ink. In the center was a leather-like case with a lock and its key, and in it a portable Brother typewriter, the base of which was hooked to a coin slide fitted for one quarter. Next to it was a square porcelain dish with a delicate painting of white birds with long necks and black curved beaks. In it were several newly minted 25 cent pieces. The first time she came she was lucky to find one quarter in the bottom of her purse's frayed lining, but now she was too frazzled to find it odd to see a handwritten note tucked under the dish, which read: "*Our sincere apologies for not providing sufficient change on your last visit. We hope you will find this supply ample.*"

The door had, as before, been unlocked. She was a bit out of breath from the climb and a little guilty for calling in sick to a job she only tolerated. "Better to be sick than late," she thought, and thought, too, of the girls whom she had left in the company of the kindly neighbor across the hall. She put down her purse and removed her scarf and coat, sat in the chair, put a quarter in and began to type. This time she wrote about Rusty leaving her and her girls in the lurch once again, and how unfair she thought it was that with every other worry and pressure she had in this life, she might actually be pregnant for the fourth time in her rapidly passing youth. She was twenty-eight, but the lines on her face made her look like ten miles of hard road. And don't get her started about how her mother was going to react. "Stop sending me more of your mistakes to take care of," her mother had written, when she sent her older twin boys, Taylor and Mike, to live with her on the farm in Oklahoma. "Boys is fine. They can help with the work, but don't be sending out any girls. Girls is trouble." It was something she had heard her whole life and she never had the strength or any measure of rebellion in her to contradict what her mother told her. Her father had died from the influenza years before, but her mother was man enough to handle the farm alone except for itinerant hired help, and now her boys, age twelve going on manhood.

She typed for what seemed like hours, and when the last of the quarters had been played out, and the typewriter stopped in mid-word, she was spent. She surveyed the pile of paper which she placed to the right of the typewriter in the basket put there for that purpose. This time she noticed there was no trash can in the room.

Signing her name on the last page with the quill pen, she pulled out a small scrap of paper from her wallet, and wrote a series of letters and numbers underneath her signature. Corrine picked up her purse and coat, and tied her scarf around her head and neck and turned on the lamp. She closed the door and walked down the hall to the stairs and did not look back. She knew by the time she got home, there would be a crème colored envelope slipped beneath the door of her tiny apartment with five crisp new twenties. It would be enough. It had to be.

Chapter II

The breath of a child is sweet and pure. Not at all like the scentless flower referred to as "baby's breath." "More like a rose," she thought. "Perhaps what heaven might smell like?"

Nora checked the boy's IV and noted his vitals on the chart and her impressions of his breathing, leaving out any particulars about the fragrance. That would be unprofessional, and above all she was a professional. She had worked at the Madison Care Facility for nearly twenty years and would not jeopardize her reputation with such frivolous observation. She had always been serious about her job as charge nurse. From the age of seven, she understood it was her God given calling to care for any person or any creature in need of her healing touch. She would bring home wounded birds and sick kittens, or friends with scraped knees and tend to them with love and gentleness and an instinct that seemed unnatural for someone so young. She was not the least bit squeamish at the sight of blood or intimidated by any illness. Her father presumed she would become a physician, like himself. Her mother predicted an interest, perhaps, in veterinarian school, something to "pass the time" until she met some nice boy, got married and had children. But because Nora read somewhere that a patient lives or dies at the hand of their nurse, this is what she chose.

She was unmarried and had no children. She did not date and had no friends, male or female. Her patients were her only concern and her only reason for living. Though she grieved more over her own failures when one of them died, she did do one small thing as an expression of sadness over the loss of her fellow man. Every Sunday, she went to church, and lit a candle for each and every person who had passed away while under her care. She had long ago set her limit at twelve. The boy lying in Madison, on the second floor, in room 317, would not become number thirteen if she had anything to say about it, but nevertheless, she was grateful for any divine intervention she might glean.

And then that Sunday, in the middle of the night, he went flat-line. Not dead. Just in limbo. He would continue to breathe but not on his own; sleep, but not dream. It was Nora's day off, so they did not call her. She found out when she returned to the hospital on Monday, and she was not pleased. He had suffered a severe stroke caused by a massive arterial rupture deep in the brain. He would not recover, and he would not die, as long as his bodily functions were looked after. So from that standpoint, Nora was satisfied her record was intact, but in her heart she blamed herself for not being there, and went over every detail of his chart and all the notes she had made, and the ones scribbled in by the doctors who passed by and barely glanced at their patients, but whose signatures must appear on the certificates of death. She had to make sure this boy did not die, and for the first time she wanted to talk with someone about how she felt, but there was no one.

Later that day, at lunchtime as she sat alone and ate her egg-salad sandwich on rye bread and drank her ice tea with lemon and no sugar, she saw the tiny, but distinct, black-bordered ad at the back of the medical journal she was reading. It was situated in between an article on the rampant use of steroids by Olympic hopefuls, and an ad for Viagra.

> *"Alone? Need someone to Confide in? Your Complete Privacy is Assured. Come One...Come All to The Typing Room! We pay good, honest Money for your Story of Isolation and Tribulation."*

"Isn't that what Confession is for?" Nora thought, and put the magazine aside as she cleared her tray from the table.

She worked a late shift and went home tired, with feet and shins and hips begging for the relief of a hot bath. As she lay in the tub with the steamy water rising around her, and the bubbles from the bath gel she indulged in (but only bought because it was a discontinued brand and therefore on sale,) she thought about the boy. His name was Alfonso and he had been at the Madison Care Facility for nearly two years. He was a ward of the state, sent there because he'd been an abused child whose mother had tried to smother him and almost succeeded, but not quite. So now he had gone from maybe waking up to merely existing. She had requested to be put full-time on his case, and the hospital administrator approved, noting for the record that no nurse had ever shown such dedication to task as Nora Poole, RN.

She slept very soundly that night, and woke refreshed and alert with a start the next morning. To mask the sound of her aloneness, she always and immediately turned on her favorite news station. Watching this show was her only source of humor, and she marveled that people could act like such fools while delivering potentially serious news. "They probably make more money in a year that I will ever see in my lifetime," she said out loud. But, of course, there was no one to hear, except for the plants, and they didn't seem to be doing all that well. She never did have much luck with plants. Perhaps they were on a different wavelength than people or animals.

After she dressed and just as she was scooping up her keys and her purse, which she always left on the table by the front door, she noticed a curious thing. The medical journal she had been reading was on the table. Only she really did not remember bringing it home with her. "Oh, well," she sighed, "I must have been more tired than I thought." So she decided to finish reading it at lunch and tucked it under her arm along with the morning paper, which she always read during the first break of the day.

As she stepped out onto the street, she realized it might rain, because the sky was turning gray and the air felt charged, and she lamented not bringing an umbrella as the comic weatherman had suggested. But Nora could see the bus coming down the block and she was not going to be late. She was never late, and more important than even this, Alfonso was waiting.

Chapter III

Jack was not exactly a loser, just hopelessly average. Average height, average build, average appearance. The kind of man people describe that way to the authorities because there is nothing special about them. They are forgettable.

Not a bad guy really, but certainly no prize. His three ex-wives would attest to that. Still, one had to admit, three women had found him charming enough to say yes, if only to wise up quickly and dump him in rapid succession because – let's face it – he was borderline boring and often pig-headed, and talked way too much for a man, and he had a rather small penis to boot. You'd never know just looking at him as he sat on the bus that less than six hours ago he had murdered his best friend, Harry, seemingly in cold blood. Nor that the worn imitation leather briefcase in his lap was chock full of tightly wrapped stacks of one-hundred-dollar bills. Now you probably would suppose that he killed said friend for the money, but that just wasn't so. His friend had asked him to, and being a good friend, Jack obliged. The money was part of the deal, and Jack took the money because why would he leave it behind for the police to take and divvy up?

He took this bus every day, because somewhere along the line he had neglected to renew his driver's license and didn't want to go to the DMV and stand in line with "all those foreigners," who in his narrow viewpoint had no business even being in this country to begin with. Now he rode the bus with them. "It's like freakin' Ellis Island in here," he thought, shifting his body to take up both seats, lest someone sit next to him. "God knows what diseases those people might have."

So, in addition to being lackluster and often obstinate, with too much to say about too little, and having a diminutive dick, Jack Hollinger was a bigot. Oh, and a possibly a murderer, and certainly a killer. There is a precise difference, however, especially if you have committed one act and not the other. Murder is the illegal act of deliberately rendering someone lifeless without their permission, whereas killing is like putting an animal, or in the case of his friend, a person, who is old and suffering, out of their misery, with permission. It's the permission part that Jack was exceedingly clear about. So that morning, with a clean conscience, he was on his way to the savings and loan where he had worked for the past six years, but where he might not work for much longer given the amount of money he was planning to put in his personal safe deposit box.

It was beginning to sprinkle, and with the windshield wipers of the bus merely spreading dirt and grime over the front window, the bus driver almost didn't see the woman standing at the next stop, but for her white hat, and white stockings and shoes, peering out from a navy blue poncho.

"Thank you, driver," said Nora, as she boarded and paid her fare. She stood at the front, making no attempt to find a seat.

"I guess she doesn't want to sit next to any of these people, either," thought Jack.

He had seen her before and knew she would be getting off two stops before his, at the hospital down the street from his office. He had never spoken to her and wasn't about to. Besides, he was too busy thinking about making a phone call to alert someone about the dead body. No use letting his friend stink up the place. After all, Harry had been a good guy and deserved to be put in the ground in a timely manner. All the burial arrangements had been made, so there was nothing left to do but wait to be notified of his best friend's demise and show up at the wake.

The rain was beginning to fall in earnest and the traffic slowed to an unhappy crawl. People around him began to look at their watches. "Probably late to their welfare office appointments." thought Jack. "Freakin' lowlifes. While the rest of us hard working, tax-paying Americans bust our humps to support them." It never occurred to him that many of the people on the bus, which was now very full, were also on their way to jobs washing dishes, or sewing garments, or cleaning houses, or caretaking children, and that being late was not an option because there was always a line of other people who would take the job for less money and not complain about the lousy working conditions. He only saw the brown skin and the brightly colored clothing and the sound of languages he did not understand and didn't care to. He peered out the glass and as the bus made its way across town, he made note of at least three languages other than English dominating the business signs in the passing neighborhoods.

He was lost in the mire of his own self-righteousness when he felt a tap on his shoulder. He looked over and into the face of a young, pregnant woman. "Por favor, Señor?" she said, motioning him to move over. For a moment he hesitated, wondering whether to stand up and let her move to the inside seat or merely scoot over and let her sit on the aisle. He quickly decided it would be better to sit by the window because this ride was obviously going to be longer than he thought and he could look out the window rather than looking into someone's rear end.

As the bus ride continued, he began to get restless. Sometimes reading the paper helped, but there was hardly enough room to fully open the front page, so he looked around for one of the pennysaver-type magazines that are always stuffed at the side of the seat or left on the floor. They always had the most interesting little notices for cheap cars and garage sales, and "how to make money by stuffing envelopes" announcements. He was thumbing through a copy when he came across an ad which had obviously been misplaced in the 'Doing Business As' section.

> *"Feeling Guilty? Wish you could Undo It? Confession is Solace for the Soul. Come One...Come All to The Typing Room! We pay good, honest Money for your Story of Self-Recrimination and Regret."*

"Shit!" said Jack, quickly clearing his throat, not that anyone was listening. He read the ad several times. It annoyed him that this ad would appear in this paper, on this bus, today of all days. He tossed the throwaway paper on the floor, and made a motion to the girl next to him to move so he could get out and make his way to the door before his stop came up. He noticed the nurse had just rung the bell for her exit and made his way to the back door. He felt kind of bad for her since it was really pouring hard and she did not have an umbrella, and he wondered if the starch in her white cap would withstand the water, but he could see as she exited that she had removed the cap and was carrying it in a plastic bag which she must have brought with her.

He exited the bus, managing to avoid getting splashed as it drove away, and walked quickly to his office around the corner. He had the one windowless private office at the back of the floor, adjacent to the safe deposit box room in the walk-in safe. Only the VPs had windows to the outside street, and everyone else sat out in the open at freestanding desks or in low-walled cubicles. It was a grand space, with ceilings some twenty feet high and velvet-draped windows nearly as tall. The ceilings were coffered in broad oak beams and had huge, crystal chandeliers hanging down from them. The floor was a black and tan and melon terrazzo with designs that looked like pinwheels, outlined in brass. There were species-size Kentia palms in enormous ceramic planters, and the desks were dark and oversized, and the chairs and sofas were overstuffed in jewel-colored brocades. The overall design was meant to convey a feeling that, if the space looked this rich, just imagine how well your money must be doing.

Jack put down his briefcase, and hung his coat at the back of the door. Because his umbrella was still wet and he did not want it to drip on the carpeting, he placed it in the trashcan at the side of his desk. He had some messages which he felt could wait, and taking his briefcase with him, went to see Miss McNamara, who was in charge of entry to the safe deposit boxes. He'd seen her arrive just after he unlocked the door to his office.

"Good morning, Elaine." Jack smiled. "I see you were prepared for the weather. May I help you with your coat?" As he spoke, she, too, placed her umbrella in a trashcan.

She nodded and smiled. "Well, it pays to be prepared, doesn't it? I always keep an umbrella in my car, just in case, though I can't remember when we had a rain like this." she said, as Jack helped her out of her coat and hung it up on the coat rack near her desk. "Who says chivalry is dead?" she said by way of a thank you. "Always so nice," she thought. "I can't imagine why he is not married." Though he gave a neutral impression, she liked polite guys, probably because so few men were. It did seem like a lost art, the observance of propriety.

"I'd like to get into my box, if you have a minute now, you know, before we get the first rush of customers?" Jack said, with a quick nod and a wink.

"No problem. Do you have your key?" She pulled out the log book where she made a note of the date and time and wrote down Jack's name and the box number from the key he showed her.

"Let me know when you're done, I'm just going to make some coffee. May I fix you a cup? I'll just leave it here on my desk when you come out."

"That would be most appreciated, I won't be but a minute." They both walked in to the safe and placed their keys in Box #2216, and simultaneously turned the keys. She turned and walked out, not completely unaware that

Jack was watching the sway of her bottom. "What I could do with that piece of ass," he purred.

When she was out of sight, he went into one of the five cell-sized rooms specifically meant for reviewing the contents of one's box, locking the door behind him. He knew his transaction was private. He'd checked that out before he ever rented a box. And he made sure when he first signed up for one that, as an employee, the integrity of his box was no different than any Joe Schmo who might come in off the street and request one. This was especially important since the S&L might not look kindly on the types of things he kept in it.

First was the flask of bourbon. It was sterling silver, engraved with his initials. A wedding gift from his first wife, Barbara. Then there was the set of naked Polaroids of wife number two. She was the most athletic of his three wives, so her leaving him was a real loss, but at least he still had the pictures, which proved quite useful in the divorce settlement negotiations. Then there was the wedding ring from wife number three. She knew he had taken it, but they were successful in making the insurance company pay up for the "loss" just before the divorce, and so she was satisfied with the money, and he was happy because he planned to someday give it to wife number four, whomever she might be.

He had counted the stacks before he left poor, dear, dead Harry, so he knew there were fifty stacks of one-hundred-dollar bills, and that each stack was worth ten thousand dollars, so Harry had paid him the tidy sum of five hundred thousand dollars to off him. Not bad for ten minutes' work.

It was a simple plan, and even simpler to make it look completely like suicide, which is what Harry had wanted. First he took all those pills. That was easy enough since Harry was a doctor and could write the prescription himself. It was a combination of sleeping pills and other drugs, which when taken with alcohol (gin was Harry's drink) would render the person pretty lifeless. But just to make sure, he wanted his best friend, Jack, to put a pillow over his face until he was like the Wicked Witch of the East: "absolutely, positively, undeniably, and reliably dead," and would not merely pass into an irreversible coma and be a stalk of broccoli for the rest of his life, which at fifty-one might be quite a long time. And to sweeten the deal, he had withdrawn all the cash he could get his hands on to have the five hundred thousand dollars which he felt was a fair price to have himself killed.

When he was done, Jack took a swig from the flask and hoped that one of the flavored creams in his coffee, waiting for him at Elaine's desk, would cover the smell. He figured that if he took a crosstown bus at lunch time, he could safely make a phone call to the cops and anonymously complain about the odor coming from the hotel suite where he and Harry had done the deed, so to speak. He had been certain to place a "Do Not Disturb" sign on the door when he left and exited down the stairs. No one noticed him enter, as the hotel had a large and well trafficked lobby, and there were no cameras in the stairwells, this being the criteria Harry and he had set some time ago when planning this whole thing out.

Anyway, the deed was done and though he was not exactly wealthy and could not buy happiness, he certainly could rent it, and made certain to ask Elaine out to dinner when he went and thanked her for the coffee.

He sat down at his desk and, seeing that his umbrellas was relatively dry, pulled it from the trash can. At the bottom, he noticed a crumpled newspaper. "Those freakin' cleaning people," he bellowed. "They're lucky to have a job, and they can't even do it right!" He pulled out the damp, smelly paper planning to throw it away in the copy room down the hall. You could have knocked him over with a feather when he saw it was the page from the paper on the bus, the one with the ad from The Typing Room.

Chapter IV

"**N**o, really, I understand. No, it's okay. You go, have a good time. Of course, I'll be fine. Aren't I always? Yeah. okay. Well, call me later? Love you. I said, I love you. Bye, now." Eleanor Sweets, or "Sweetie" as she liked to be called, made her decision the very second she hung up the phone. He was not coming over. He had to take his daughter to some kind of school event. Of course his wife, from whom he was estranged, but not yet separated, would be there too, even if Sweetie's lover, Roan, did not mentioned the fact. Sweetie went to the bulletin board in the kitchen where she had pinned up the ad. She had seen it three times, once on the community bulletin board at the Laundromat, once at the corner market, and once at the gym where she worked out four days a week. She was thirty-three, and for the past seven years, she had been utterly and quite hopelessly in love with this man, almost as long as he had been married. Now, since she had taken a vacation day to spend it with a lover who had better things to do, she decided, it might be time to find out what this place in the ad was all about. She could barely read the address. So fine was the print, she had to put on her glasses, which she seldom did in public because she was too vain. But in the privacy of her kitchen, standing nude except for one of the many silk robes Roan had bought her over the years, she slipped them on and read the ad once more.

> *"Is your Love Life at a Dead End? Are you on the Losing End of an Affair? Come One...Come All to The Typing Room! We pay good, honest Money for your Tale of Heartache and Betrayal."*

She took a cab because she did not want her car to be seen anywhere near this place, whatever it was. "1242 Kenmore Road? This is it, lady," said the cab driver, as he pulled over to the curb. The rain had stopped as quickly as it began, and the sun was now shining brightly through dispersing clouds. She took note that the street was lined with trees planted in tight circular wrought-iron fences and there was a little park on the other side. It must have been one of the better neighborhoods at one time, but had taken on the air of shabbiness that sometimes comes when owners are moving out and tenants are moving in. A place in transition. But still, there were flowers in the flower boxes, and the street was swept and clean, and although the park had probably seen better days, it must be safe because there were people wiping the benches to sit and have lunch, and walking dogs, and watching over children in their strollers. "So, probably there are no weirdos up there," she thought as she surveyed the building from the street, looking up to the top floor.

The ad said Apartment 4-F. There was no elevator, which was a bit inconvenient since she was wearing rather high heels. "Come fuck me shoes," is what Roan called them. Why she even bothered to wear them today was not a completely unconscious choice. She was, in her way, saying fuck you to Roan. Fuck you, for not coming to see me today. Fuck you, for not getting a divorce. Fuck you, for not loving me more than her. That was really what she was upset about. He did not love her enough to make it official. So they could be seen together in public. So that they could make plans, without fear of interruption from children, and school projects, and business meetings, and social events, and wives. So they would have the same measure of spontaneity enjoyed by other couples. But they were not a couple. There was Roan and all his baggage, and then there was Sweetie.

It was seven years ago, and Roan had been married for only six months when he met her. It was her first day at the marketing firm where he had just been made a junior executive. Oh, but he had ambitious plans, where visions of a corner office, designer furniture, a newer, more expensive car with a reserved parking space and executive VP titles played in his head. He'd recently married his wife, whom he loved, particularly since she was influential in getting him noticed for the promotion, having been at the firm herself since college. Things couldn't be better or his future brighter.

"It's a great place to work,' said Pam, the young woman who was giving Sweetie a tour of the office before taking her to the secretarial pool. "Actually, it's called the "Assistants Division," Talk about marketing something, huh?" She said with a wink. "But you look like you could go far, ah, "Sweetie" is it? I bet the guys just love that!" she laughed. "I will say this; just between us girls...it's amazing how far a good blow job can take you in this place, if you know what I mean." She didn't exactly lower her voice, so

Sweetie was a little embarrassed, but her tour guide didn't seem to notice. "Anyway, here you are," she announced, as they reached her desk. "You'll be working for Mr. Fitzpatrick. He's young, cute and very upwardly mobile, if you get my drift. But don't worry, because he just got married and his wife works here, too." Pam wrote down her extension and mentioned something about lunch later or drinks after work and went down the hall without hearing if Sweetie was interested in either. "All that was missing was her snapping her gum," she thought.

Just as she was settling in at her workspace which was really a very small cubicle, with a chair that seemed to be broken, she surveyed the piles of paper on her desk and wondered if she had been led to the wrong place. "I just got here," she whined. "They can't expect me to do all this work the first day!"

"That depends on how late you can stay tonight," said a voice from behind.

She turned and looked into the face of the man she, in the years that followed, would work for, and yearn for, and make love to, and cry over. Only now she was all cried out.

She wasn't sure if going to this place and talking with someone would help. But she felt there must be some kind of kismet going on to have seen this ad in so many places, especially since Roan had been canceling more often of late. Like this morning when he called from his cell phone on the way to the kid's school. "Sorry, my girl, but I have obligations I just can't turn my back on. It's not like I ever lied to you about them, so let's just plan on spending more time together this weekend. You sure you'll be okay? You know I'd rather be with you. That's my Sweetie. You sure you're okay? Oh, and I'm having something sexy sent over just for you, doll. I know you'll look great in it. Can't wait to peel it off you. What's that, oh, yeah, love you, too, babe. Gotta run. Bye."

Why do men always sound so distracted when they are breaking a promise to you? Shouldn't they be more focused as they tear out your heart? Doesn't Roan know I already have more fuckin' let-me-see-you-in-this-outfit-for-ten-seconds-before-I-jump-your-bones-clothes than even Heidi Fleiss would ever need to own? Why are they so thoughtless? "Why am I so stupid?" She asked herself as she knocked on the door to the apartment. There was no answer.

She knocked again, a bit louder this time. No answer. "Oh, fine. I've come all this way, and there's no one here." But she tried the door handle and was surprised to find it unlocked. "Okay, maybe there's some kind of waiting area," she thought as she let herself in.

Instead she found herself in a single room with no one in it. "Hello," she called out, and then felt silly when she realized there were no other doors leading to this room, so there couldn't be anyone coming out from some other part of the apartment. This room was the apartment. "Well, maybe they've just stepped out," she said to herself. "I'll wait a few minutes and if no one comes, I'll just go home and order a pizza, and watch a movie. A sad movie, and have a good cry." She surveyed the classic, elegant furnishings, the fine Oriental rug, and the upholstered walls, and noted how pleasant the room was, its sparseness somehow soothing. She sat down at the only chair in the room, in front of the desk by the window. On the desk was a rather antiquated typewriter. She hadn't seen a typewriter in a very long time. PCs had rendered them virtually useless except on rare occasions when you were filling out a form which had not been scanned into your hard drive. And yet it seemed to fit this room. A laptop would actually seem out of place here.

Looking at her watch, she wondered if indeed someone would be coming back. Just as she was thinking about leaving, she saw an envelope sitting on top of a stack of expensive typing bond, to the left of the machine. On it was written *"Miss Eleanor Sweets."*

At first she smiled, the way you do when you recognize something safe and familiar like your own name, but just as quickly, she frowned and then began to panic. "Who knows I was coming here?" She frowned and stood up to look out the window to the street below. She didn't see anything different from up here than she had seen when she exited the cab earlier. The street was sunny and there were people out walking, and cars driving by, and the scene at the park across the street was still giving the impression of a carefree afternoon. There had been no phone number on the ad, just the address and a series of numbers and letters. She took the ad out of her purse and looked at it again. No phone number, and there was no phone in the room.

"That's it, I'm outta here," she said and went to the door and was relieved to find it still unlocked and was just about to leave when she thought about the envelope. It had her name on it, so she felt she should at least take it with her, that way there would not be anything to connect her to this place. She'd figure out later how anyone would know she had planned on coming here. But right now she just wanted to get as far away as possible. If it was going to be fight or flight, she'd rather get the hell out of there.

She walked across the room and reached for the envelope. The script was rather artistic, though not stiff like calligraphy. More like someone who got an "A" in penmanship, when they used to teach that in grade school. She remembered how her grandmother used to have lovely handwriting. "Funny, I haven't thought about her in ages," she whispered to herself. People today don't write as often as they type, and they certainly don't practice to write in a style that is both refined and distinguished. Most people she knew actually printed rather than wrote in longhand, so there was something compelling about the envelope with her name so elegantly penned.

She stood at the desk and with the index finger of her perfectly polished porcelain nails, slid open the seal on the envelope flap. Inside were two pages, all handwritten, in the same graceful writing:

> *Dear Miss Sweets,*
>
> *I trust you had no trouble finding our establishment. We hope the drama of our little ad did not offend in any way, but if you are reading this, we know you must be at the point in your current situation to share your story, perhaps in the very real hope of coming to a clear-cut resolution.*
>
> *Because your well-being is our first priority, we take pride in providing a space that is comfortable, but not intrusive, so your thoughts and feelings have a space free from commotion and interruption. We understand these elements might be of particular concern to you.*

As our ad stated, we pay a sum of money, commensurate with the tale we trust you will now be comfortable sharing with us. Everyone comes here alone, but each and every visitor leaves with the assurance that their story will find a home in our hearts and minds, and no further. Your confidentiality is assured. And more important, you will have the calm and serenity which comes in knowing your plea for an answer will be heard. Sometimes that is all we really need, isn't it? A shoulder to cry on. A kind word of declaration that we are not alone in how we feel, or what we think, or even what we may have done. If you please, then, Miss Sweets, take a seat and tell us your story. When you are done, please place the pages in the basket. Do not be the least bit concerned about any corrections; we understand. Spare no detail. The more specific the story, the more we have to work with.

We ask you use the pen provided, not the pencil, if you please, and sign your name at the end of the last page. And please write in the code from the ad which brought you to us. If you would be so kind as to also, please, turn on the lamp just before you leave.

When you return to your home, you will find compensation in the prescribed manner. The rest will come in due time.

Thank you for coming today, Miss Sweets. If you find satisfaction in the arrangement, you are welcome to return anytime.

Sincerely,

The Typing Room

Chapter V

Sweetie plopped down in the chair. She wasn't sure if she needed a drink, or if she was going to be ill. And she really could not understand why she did not just run out of the room screaming. But instead, she sat. She read the letter again, and once more after that.

"Who are these people? How do they know so much about me? How I feel about things?"

She thought about everything that had happened in the last few years. About Roan, and about their relationship, what she had sacrificed for him. The wasted time and the lost opportunities she had willingly given up to be with him. There was the job transfer to New York, a city she had always dreamed of living in, and a chance at a career and not just a job. The home she did not have, children she did not have, the husband she did not have. In exchange for what? A few afternoons a month, when it was convenient, in an apartment she paid for because she was too proud to let him set her up. "That would mean I was your mistress, like I was nothing special. I love you, and I choose to be with you." She tried to explain to him. In her new king-sized bed with pale pink silk sheets, or on the bondage black leather sofa he had arranged to reimburse her for with cash at first left on the nightstand, but later, when he saw how she reacted, into a bank account she could draw from. And the time he managed to get away on some business trip, and they spent a long weekend in San Francisco, acting like a young couple in love, pretending they were on holiday with not a care or consideration in the world. A furtive conversation on a cell phone which almost ended everything because he mistakenly brought the bill home in a pile of paperwork from his office and the wife just happened to see it. "Oh, honey, that's nothing, I just had to call her to check on a file she took home to work on. That's all." The hour she once spent at a restaurant waiting for him, only to get a message from the maître d' which read "So sorry, babe. Something came up. Will drop by later. R." All these things and a whole lot more. Seven years' worth of things.

For the next two hours she typed, putting in quarter after quarter, taken from the little dish that sat next to the typewriter. She didn't bother to wipe away the tear drops that stained the ink as they fell onto the paper. And when she was done, she left the pages in the basket as the letter had instructed her to. She signed her name with the quill pen, and wrote the code from the ad which she put her glasses on to see. She turned on the lamp and shut the door behind her. She put the ad and the letter in her purse, and pulling out her cell phone, called for a cab, which was conveniently waiting for her by the time she walked down the four flights of stairs and on down the steps to the street.

She opened the back window all the way down and breathed deeply for the first time in months, wanting a cigarette, but deciding that was something else she planned on giving up. The city had been washed clean from the rain, and with her visit to The Typing Room, so was her spirit. When she got home, and as she opened up the door to her apartment, she found a crème-colored envelope, and inside were twenty crisp, one-hundred-dollar bills.

Chapter VI

The morning went by without incident. In medical terms that meant no hearts, lungs or bowels ceased to function. Everything and everyone was on schedule. This made Nora happy or what most people would find simply acceptable, but not really cheerful. In any case, the morning had gone smoothly, and more importantly, she was able to spend time taking care of Alfonso, the young boy in the now CAT Scan-confirmed irreversible coma.

Lucky for this patient, she had had extensive experience in taking care of comatose or otherwise vegetative cases. For the last eight years of her nursing career, she had specialized in geriatrics, the care of old people. Most of them were like children in many ways. They needed to be coached on when to get up, and what to wear, and what to eat and when, and sometimes even how to chew and swallow their food, and when to use the facilities, or what to do if they couldn't, and she was adept at how to deal with poor, frightened and confused beings who quite often did not understand what you were saying, and couldn't respond to even the simplest of questions, because many had lost the capacity to know they were even alive.

These patients were the ones who made her especially sad, because they were a reminder of the sign post we all fear seeing at the end of our journey through life. The one that says "Detour," putting you on a road not shown on the map. The one that takes you away from a comfortable retirement on the beach in Florida, or by the pool in Palm Springs, or in the Keno lounge in Las Vegas, waiting for the next floor show, with one of those festive umbrella drinks in one hand and your well-worn slot-machine card in the other. The one where you are existing, but not living. And mostly you appear to be sleeping, but really you just don't want to be reminded that you are still here in this body, the one that will not move when you want it to, the one that lies in the hospital bed, getting stiffer and more sore-ridden by the day, and thinner and more fragile by the week, and lonelier and more anxious by the month and the years that seem to stretch out forever.

No, she'd had her fill of taking care of the old. The senile and the ones with Alzheimer's were just too much for her to bear. Though several of her patients were still alive and doing surprisingly well, because the nursing staff at Madison was the best in the city, she was glad to be taking care of the young ones now. They, at least, gave her some hope. All of them, except Alfonso. So she felt it was her duty to give him some, or at least a measure of kindness and a level of caretaking which would demonstrate to him in whatever way he might perceive it, and if only at a visceral level, that he had not been abandoned, though, like the aged, he seemed to have abandoned her.

So today, she found herself talking to him, more than usual. She told him about the rain in the morning, and how she forgot her umbrella, the ride on the bus, and the fact that she liked to stand at the front, and though she, quite naturally, did not like feeling pressed in by people she did not know, she did so that she might get a good view of where she was going. Always prepared for an emergency, Nora was the one person you would want near you in a crisis because she was so even-tempered and had great ballast in both girth and temperament. However, she did not like surprises. They disrupted the routine. And all good nursing depended on maintaining a routine.

Keeping to a schedule allowed every patient to be well fed, and bathed and dressed on time to sit up in the day room, if that is what was called for. In fact, the laws concerning the care of the infirm were very clear that a patient, except those who were hooked up to some kind of life-support mechanism, or those for whom excessive movement might be harmful, must be moved out of their room and into some sort of stimulating environment, though how many of them would have the wherewithal to perceive such a change was unknown. Maybe the administration just wanted to get them out of the room, to make it easier for the janitors to keep up with their work, and most certainly to make the family members, who did on occasion come to visit, feel like their loved one might somehow be on the road to recovery. It gave some of them hope, and others such a sense of continuing loss that eventually they would stop coming.

Not that Nora had completely abandoned her former charges. Though they were in a different wing of the hospital, sometimes on her way to the lab to check personally on the status of a test, or to accompany a particularly anxious patient to his next area of treatment, she would stop by and pay them a visit. "Hello, my dears,"

Nora would say to them as they sat or lounged in the day room. "How are you today?" She would smooth their hair, or straighten a collar or button a sweater, and fluff a pillow, or reposition their wheelchairs or day beds so they could get a better view outside the window. Did they even see that it was a beautiful day, that the sky was now blue and that the clouds, once filled with rain, were now wispy and white?

The newer patients called out to her for some attention, and she was actually happy to oblige, though she did not choose to stay for very long because it might upset the nurses who were in charge on this floor. She was like some visiting general, and did not want to intimidate the troops by lingering. There were only five of her original patients left as the rest of them had died and two had been transferred to private nursing facilities. Nora never counted these dead ones against her record, because death as one approaches eighty or ninety is, after all, ultimately unavoidable. The trick is to go quickly and with little or no pain. The worst was to linger and suffer in silence.

Chapter VII

What if Harry wasn't dead? If one were a first-year philosophy student, one might say this was an interesting metaphysical conundrum, but right now this thought, having plagued Jack since he saw that soggy paper in the trash can, was beginning to give his stomach a perfectly awful churning sensation. No, it was really quite a physical problem which barely contained itself until he got to the men's room and lost all of his breakfast and the coffee he had shared with Elaine.

"Damn it!" he said, as he washed up at the sink and inspected his jacket and tie and shirt for any signs or smells that would give evidence to his recent face-to-face encounter with the toilet in stall number three.

What if he wasn't really dead? Maybe I left too soon. Maybe he didn't take enough of those pills. Maybe he was just barely breathing, and after I left, decided he'd made a mistake, and managed to crawl to the phone and call for help? The panic was beginning to rise in his mind, only to blurt out, "Oh, God, what if he fingers me for botching the job?"

Not wanting to draw attention to himself by leaving earlier, at exactly 12:01 p.m., he left for lunch to make the phone call about Harry, and find out if his fears were at all founded in fact. He exited the crosstown bus and looked around for a phone booth from which he would not draw attention. Locating one was proving to be more difficult than he thought. Most people are practically hard-wired to their cell phones, so more and more of the phone booths one used to find in abundance outside of office buildings or near corner stores were becoming extinct.

And since this particular bus had placed him in a more residential part of the city, his task was even trickier. But within a block, he found a small park and in it was an old-fashioned phone booth. This one was built to look like the large, red, wooden English phone booths. It even had a little seat.

He decided once more on the bus ride over, that he could simply call the hotel to complain about what by now must be an obnoxious odor coming from Suite 1111, and so he placed the call and waited for the front desk clerk to answer. Then he hung up. What if Harry was dead after all, and they somehow traced this particular call to an outside number, and that the call, having not come from within the hotel itself, was probably from the guy who murdered poor Harry! "Jeez, this is getting more complicated by the minute," said Jack.

On the other hand, there was no way to connect him with having made that particular call at that particular moment in time. He looked around and took comfort from the fact that no one was the least bit interested in his activities, or even his very existence. Somehow that was not an insult. In fact, he was used to it.

"Maybe I should just forget the call entirely, and let the maid find him."

He was positive the "Do Not Disturb" sign would eventually be ignored, either that or someone else would make a legitimate complaint about any foul smell, and Harry would be found. Which brought him back to the question, was Harry really dead? And if Harry was dead, who was leaving him these ads with the implication that he, Jack, had done something wrong in the first place? He reminded himself that the whole thing was, from the beginning, Harry's bright idea.

"I can't go through that, Jack, it would be worse than being buried alive, I tell you," said Harry, a week ago today, over drinks at their favorite watering hole, The Twisted Nail Tavern.

"Maybe the tests are wrong, Harry. I mean, isn't that why you guys call it 'practicing' medicine? Maybe you need a second opinion," said Jack, on his second bourbon neat, to Harry on his third gin and tonic.

"I already did that. The PET was pretty conclusive and so were all the other tests. If I don't do something now, while I still can, you will be wiping drool from my mouth when you come to see me. You'd come by to visit me, wouldn't you, Jack?"

"Sure, Harry, of course I would. But why are we talking about that when you seem set on doing this other thing? I mean, if you're serious about it and all."

"Listen, I know what I have to do, and I want to know you'll do your share. I have to believe being dead is better than it would be to sit there like some kind of turnip on the road to being dead, but never getting picked up for the ride, you know what I mean?"

"Yeah, I guess so."

"And don't get me started about all the other people who got it and didn't bail. I don't give a flying rat's ass about what they did and why. Maybe they were braver, or more God-fearing or maybe they were too scared to make a move. But I know I can't do this and I'm counting on you, so don't fuck this up for me, old pal. Just think of this as the last wish of a dying man and think of the money as just a token of my thanks. You know, so you won't feel bad about doing it."

"Yeah, okay."

And so the conversation went.

Which brought him right back to the nagging question, was Harry dead or wasn't he? "Fuck it," thought Jack, deciding to go back to work. "What's the worst that could happen? He's dead and there's no harm, no foul; or he's alive and incapable of naming names, so I'm in the clear, either way." In fact, Jack was already thinking about how he should react when he got the news, whatever it was.

Just as he was leaving the park, he looked over at a young attractive blonde in very high heels getting into a cab across the street. "Whoa, what a knockout! Wonder who she was giving some afternoon delight to?" And Jack turned the corner to catch the bus. It was then he noticed the street sign "Kenmore Road" and realized, with the same queasy feeling he had this morning, that this was the street mentioned in the annoying little ad which seemed to be stalking him.

Chapter VIII

"**W**here does the money really come from?" He asked The Proprietress. "I'm curious why no one makes a fuss about what is missing. "

"They know the money is not theirs to begin with, so to whom would they complain? Besides," she continued, "the people who 'contribute' the money are not the type to go to the authorities and raise any suspicion."

"Oh, so you mean drug dealers?"

"Well, yes," she said. "They've been the primary source, but there are others. Hit men, government officials on the take, errant lottery winners who waste their blessing on hookers and exotic dancers, people who, in general, get money they are not entitled to or who choose to waste the money they do have in ways that decent people would find most objectionable."

"Have any of them come here? You know, to confess?"

"None we advertised for, specifically, though many have come for other reasons, to be sure, and we find out about the money that way."

"I still don't get it. Exactly how do you make the 'withdrawal'? And how does it get to the intended recipient? Is that what the code is for?"

She was beginning to get annoyed with him. After all, he was just passing through now and she did not feel the least bit compelled to reveal any more than she had to.

Especially to someone who should not be here in the first place. People of his ilk did not have quite the same dedication to the work required and besides they, like this one, asked too many questions and took time away from the real purpose for them all being gathered together.

"Why don't you stop pestering me about this," she finally said. "I've told you all I'm going to."

He sensed she was someone to be reckoned with. Of course he had no way to know, but there was a time when she had a well-deserved reputation for standing up to trouble whenever it was stupid enough to get in her way. Once, not long after her husband of many years had passed away, she was leaving her local bank. Being the last customer that afternoon, and with the parking lot nearly empty, the security guard offered to walk her to her car, which was parked in the shade several lanes away from the door. Although she politely declined, he waited until she was standing at her car door. She waved and he waved and he went into the bank, locking the door behind him, as she opened the door to her new emerald green 1974 Chevrolet Camaro Z28

Now this was quite a bit of car for anybody, but especially for a widow nearing her 60th birthday, but it was the first real purchase she had made on her own and she was very proud of it. And so, tossing her purse behind the passenger seat, she sat behind the wheel and fastened her seat belt, and as she turned to pull the door closed, came face to face with a small-caliber hand gun and, as she later described him, "a scruffy looking young man" who, in rather broken English, demanded her money. It was one of those moments a person is better off rehearsing for so as not to panic and screw it up. You know the kind you look back on and later think how it seemed to pass in slow motion? But she did not panic, or feel afraid for her life, or crumble or cry, nor dwell at all on her dearly departed husband except for one fleeting moment to decide it was partly his fault this was happening, because how dare he die and leave her all alone when the world is such a cold, cruel place.

Instead she got angry. So angry, in fact, that she began to scream at the young man and, pressing both hands on the steering wheel, blared the horn loudly in bursts as she hollered and pounded and cursed. She was like some madwoman, and either it was his first attempt at a robbery, or she was so frightening a visage, he decided it wasn't worth it, tucked the gun back in the front of his jeans, pulled down his shirt and made a beeline for the street.

He was not the least bit concerned with this crazy old lady, expect perhaps now he would have to rob someone else, until he felt a sharp pain at the back of his head, and then another one on his shoulder. He turned around to see her standing outside her car hurling, with blinding accuracy, the smooth black stones used as a landscape design element in the garden and lawn areas beneath the trees and bushes where he had been lying in wait for her.

Like the Biblical David, she launched another one, hitting him squarely in the forehead and when he felt the warmth that was his own blood, he thought about shooting her, but realized he was not that good a shot, and decided to run for it. He did not expect what happened next. She later told the police when they asked her why she did it, "I

41

guess I just wanted to teach him a lesson, I don't think I really wanted to kill him or anything." (Though she later confessed to her daughter, "So help me, I wanted to run him over, I was that infuriated.") She got in her car and revved the engine, burning rubber as she crossed the parking lot to chase the pathetically unsuccessful robber, who by now was running for his life. She chased him down the street, screaming and blowing her horn, until he ran down an alley and jumped over a fence, never, she was sure, to attempt another robbery anytime soon.

When she got home, the police were sitting in the driveway waiting to take a report, having only heard the bank guard's side of the story that one of their patrons was trying to run down some pedestrian. They had quite a laugh over coffee and pastry, and did not see the need to press charges, but did warn her about taking the law into her own hands. When the family heard the story at Sunday brunch, her son-in-law promptly dubbed her "The Vigilante" after the character in the latest Charles Bronson movie.

Unquestionably, she'd had quite a life.

No way would she allow this interloper to ruin what was left of it.

Chapter IX

Jack returned to his office half-expecting to see a police car parked in front of the building. He even thought about asking for a transfer and going on home to wait for them there. It would be far too embarrassing being handcuffed and taken away in front of all those people. "Wait, a minute," he asked himself, "What am I thinking here?"

He sat down at his desk and since there were no messages from either the police or Harry, decided the best thing to do would be to carry on as if all was normal, which it still seemed to be, in spite of his increasing anxiety. If only the ad didn't seem to be staring at him from way down deep in the trash can where he had left it, too unnerved to throw it away, where maybe someone else might see it and make, by some unfathomable stretch of the imagination, a connection between it and Jack and what may or may not have happened to Harry.

It was all too much to take. He needed a drink, but thought it unwise to be absent too long from his desk, for fear that the authorities called or dropped by for a chat, so a trip to the Twisted Nail was out of the question. He asked Elaine once more for access to his safe deposit box, and once ensconced in the privacy of the viewing room, took a rather large gulp from his flask, so large in fact that he would need to refill it tonight. He slipped the slim silver container in his breast coat pocket and thanked God it was not casual Friday when he might have been wearing something less concealing, Jack took a peek at several of the Polaroids, and wondered if he should, just in case, take three or four of the stacks of money. He might need to make a quick getaway to Mexico, or wherever else people who have committed reprehensible crimes go to escape justice. "No," he thought, "maybe Canada. At least they speak English there."

Then he noticed the wrapper on one of the stacks had been broken. He thought back for a moment to when he had earlier removed each of them from his briefcase and placed them neatly in the box. He was certain he would have noticed if any of them were torn, and then his innards began to sour, this time from the combination of the bourbon on an empty stomach and the growing terror that somehow, someway, someone had taken two thousand dollars from one of the stacks.

"What the fuck is going on here?"

He was about to call Elaine into the room, when he wisely decided this was definitely not the thing to do. His mind began to wander to one of those old Perry Mason episodes, and he was on the witness stand being questioned by Hamilton Burger.

"So tell the court, Mr. Hollinger, you say your friend Harry 'gave' you the money to suffocate him, is that right?"

"Yes, that's correct, we had a deal."

"I see. The prosecution rests, Your Honor."

In the daydream, Jack looked over and instead of Raymond Burr sitting at the defense table; it was Woody

Allen wearing the android costume from "Sleeper," holding up the ad from the paper.

He was doomed.

And suddenly there was a knock at the door. "Jack, I'm so sorry to disturb you, but you have an urgent telephone call." It was Elaine. "Do you want me to put your box back for you?"

"Ah, no, that's fine. I'm done here. Just tell whoever it is I'll be right there."

He shut the box and when he had replaced it, went out to his office and picked up the phone.

"Hello?"

"Mr. Hollinger?" said a female voice. There was a great deal of noise in the background.

"Yes, this is Jack Hollinger. Who is this?"

"I'm sorry to tell you this, sir, but I'm calling from the Madison Care Facility. We have a patient who was brought in several hours ago, and we found your business card and home number amongst his personal effects. Do you know a Dr. Harold Pickles?"

"Harry. Yes, I do. Ah, what seems to be the problem?" Jack spoke in as casual a voice as he could render, in spite of the fact he was really beginning to feel the need to visit stall number three again.

"Well, sir, he was brought into our emergency entrance as a possible suicide attempt. We've determined there is no family member to call, so we were wondering if, since you seem to be the only person who might have an interest in his condition, if you wouldn't mind coming down to speak with the attending physician, and give a statement to the police."

"What's that? Police you say? Why would I have to speak with them?"

"Well, Mr. Hollinger, that part is just routine. Actually, you might not even need to speak with them depending on what the doctor puts in the report."

"I see. Well, hmm, I don't know, it's rather short notice."

"It would just take a few minutes of your time, and it would help us process his paperwork so we can get him out of the ER. I see from your card, you are just a few blocks away. Is it at all possible for you to come over?"

Jack looked at his watch. It was nearing three o'clock. He figured he had time to go to the hospital, check things out, go to the American Express Travel office down the street, buy a one-way ticket on the first flight out to Tahiti (Canada was too cold this time of year,) come back to the office and empty out his safe deposit box, and be *persona absentia* before anyone was the wiser. He could write to his boss about his friend's harrowing experience and that he had decided life was too short not to live, live, live, so would they mind too terribly much and just take their job and stick it where the sun routinely did not shine.

"Well, certainly, I can. Anything for ol' Harry. Suicide you say?"

"Yes, sir, it looks that way. The toxicology report is not back yet, but we're pretty sure. Anyway, he's stable."

"Stable? Does that mean he's conscious?" Jack said, and thought he might have to change his plans a bit and go straight to the travel agency.

"Oh, no, I'm afraid he's comatose at the moment. Really, Mr. Hollinger, I think you should speak with the doctor in charge of his case. I'm not really at liberty to tell you much more over the phone."

"Okay, then. I'll be over as soon as I can."

"Thank you, sir. Just ask for Dr. Patterson when you get here."

"Will do."

"Oh, and sir?"

"Yes?"

"I'm sorry about your friend."

"Yeah, me too," said Jack as he hung up the phone. "Me, too."

Chapter X

Nora had decided that morning to work an extended shift and was just settling down to a late lunch. It was not like her to alter her nursing duty schedule, but when it came to her own time, she was quite free to pick and choose how late to stay or when to take a break. After she had returned from the East Wing where her former patients were housed, she spent most of the day with Alfonso. He looked so peaceful, and for reasons only a full-time caretaker, or perhaps a mother might notice, he seemed more relaxed when she was around him. She had no experience with the latter, but she knew from her years of nursing, that patients get used to the sound of someone's voice or the feel of their touch even if they do not seem to have any casually observable measure of reaction to the outside stimuli.

She also knew that comatose and even dying patients slept even if they often gave that same appearance but were really quite conscious. So when she sensed Alfonso was taking a nap, she decided to go down to the cafeteria and eat her lunch and finish reading her medical journal.

The area where the staff was designated to eat was busy as usual, because the hospital operated around the clock and so every hour was somebody's lunch period. Still, she was able to get a small table to herself in a relatively quiet zone, away from the aides, who chattered away in their many lyrical languages, or the fresh-faced female nurses who huddled together and gossiped about the young, male residents, all of whom are handsome by the very nature of their jobs, or the crying family members who sniffled with each bite of their apple pie and grilled cheese sandwiches and hot cocoa. Nora wondered why they called it comfort food.

While she ate, she often read a daily newspaper, the latest best-seller or one of her endless supply of medical journals. She liked to keep up with what was happening in the world even if she herself was not that keen on being involved with the world that went on around her. That buffer was supplied by the extreme types of books she preferred; light-hearted romance and grisly murder mysteries. And since her singular passion in life was her patients, she kept up on the most current medical news. Anything which might help her care for them more prudently.

The article on the steroid problem in athletic competitions was interesting enough, not that she was the least bit sympathetic to anyone who had been graced from above with a body which could, like a gazelle, leap the tallest barrier or swim like a dolphin or run with the speed and courage of a cheetah. She thought they were foolish. And she was troubled knowing that Alfonso would not do any of these things. He would simply lie there until time wore him away, like the Sphinx.

She tried to picture him running and playing and how mischievous his smile probably was. His lips were full and she kept them moist with a frequent application of vitamin E ointment. They were more visible now that the ventilator was functioning through a permanent tracheotomy at his slender throat. She would brush his dark coarse hair, and trim his nails, and massage and flex his arms and legs to keep them from becoming rigid, preventing the fetal curl so common in comatose patients. All these things she did for him because in her own way, she loved Alfonso very much. He was the child she would never have. And when she found herself thinking too much about what the future might hold, she would will herself to block him out of her mind, so the aloneness she felt would not take root and ruin a perfectly good bowl of chicken noodle soup at lunch, or a good night's sleep later when she returned to her empty apartment.

Nora was just about to finish her lunch and return to her floor when she again noticed the strange little ad.

"Alone? Need someone to Confide in? Your Complete Privacy is Assured. Come One...Come All to The Typing Room! We pay good, honest Money for your Story of Isolation and Tribulation."

She was a bit miffed. How dare someone advertise for stories which certainly must be very personal and sensitive, and to use the hook of money to obtain them. Who would do such a despicable thing? And what did they do with the stories? Publish them in some lurid tell all tabloid along with new reports of alien abduction or celebrities with webbed feet, or post them on one of those Internet chat rooms for other people to feed on and laugh at? And moreover, what kind of person would sell themselves so cheaply or be taken in by such a carnival sideshow-natured ad? She did not understand what motivated most people to willingly debase the temple which was their body, and their soul, mind and spirit, all of which were sacred and holy in her humble opinion. She'd seen so-called reality TV once. "It's no better than the Romans going to the Coliseum and watching the Christians being torn apart by wild beasts!" she had decided. "It's disgusting."

Obviously, she was not a fan.

She wondered, too, how an ad of this type even got printed in a well-respected medical journal, thinking it belonged in some low-brow magazine right next to the ads where Madame Zardoz promises to lift a gypsy curse, read your Tarot cards, your palm and horoscope and as a special $19.95 offer, give you a magic potion to bring back a long-lost love.

"I guess money does speak louder than good taste," she said under her breath. But the words 'alone' and 'isolation' brought a lump to her throat just the same.

As a child, Nora spent a great deal of time in her own company. Her mother was the progressive type of woman who, in the 1950s, had a job outside the home, though not a paying one, which involved her in various charities, mostly for children of third-world countries or inner-city areas neither of which anyone in her family would ever see the need to visit. She developed an insatiable capacity for reading and a knack for keeping to herself, until that first time she found a baby sparrow which had fallen from its nest. She had been told by all the sensible adults in the house that such creatures were best put out of their misery by either twisting their necks and killing them quickly, or leaving them to the elements to die painlessly by starvation or exposure. Nora was both horrified and deeply disturbed that anyone could do these terrible things to something so weak and defenseless and yet she knew they didn't see it that way at all. It was just common sense to let nature take its course, but since she had been the recipient of her mother's soothing touch and her father's expert medical care when she was sick or injured, she decided to pass this experience on to this small bird and nurse it back to health. No one was more pleased than Nora when one day it flew from her hand to the open window in her bedroom, and then on to the tree outside and then away to wherever sparrows congregate.

She was done eating, and after cleaning her table and tossing the trash, she left the magazine on the table for someone else to enjoy. When she returned to her floor, she checked in at the desk and noticed a flag on the front of Alfonso's chart. It must have been placed there by one of the aides who still did check on him when they were in the ward, but who left most of the other care duties to Nurse Poole as she had requested. It indicated a possible fever spike and noted his most recent temperature, taken when Nora was on lunch break, at 101.3 degrees Fahrenheit. This was not good. It meant he had contracted some type of infection, though nothing was outwardly apparent. And so at best, they would have to put him on a series of powerful antibiotics to combat what might be life-threatening, and at worst, threaten his life by performing exploratory surgery. Neither option was desirable for someone in his delicate condition.

He was so fragile, and so helpless.

Like her first sparrow.

Chapter XI

"What are we going to do with him?" one of them asked her. "Isn't he a bit young for our group?"

"Of course, he won't stay. Why would they send a kid here, of all places?" Another voice spoke.

"I'm not taking care of any damn kid! My own kids hardly ever come to see me and when they do they just whine and moan about how expensive it is to keep me there," said yet another one. "I'm almost afraid one of them will take a pillow to my face."

"I wouldn't count on it, if I were you." he said. "Speaking from my own experience, sometimes that doesn't work out the way you want it to, you know? And then, guess what, you're stuck here."

"How can you say such terrible things?" another one asked. "My Walter and his children come all the time. They are as pleasant and loving as they can be under the circumstances. Why, just yesterday they brought me flowers and sang songs to me, and showed me pictures," she said brightly.

"Of course, I can't smell the flowers or sing along with them, and my eyesight isn't what it used to be, but I love them for it all the same," she said more softly. "I love it when they come."

"How do they even know you can see or hear them?" the one with the cost-conscious offspring chided. "You just sit there like a lawn ornament. I bet after a while they will stop coming and then you'll see just how much they really don't care."

"That's enough," said The Proprietress in a most tolerant tone. "This child's being here is obviously an error which will work itself out at the appropriate time. In the interim, let's not frighten him more than he must be already. All of you just settle down. And as for you, Mr. Voice of Experience, you are the one who shouldn't be here. No doubt, your place is down the road apiece. Certainly it isn't here, and not for long if I have anything to say about it! So just shut your yap and stay out of my way."

"Fine,' he said with equal scorn. "So when exactly can I get out of this chickenshit organization? And where is it you intend to send me off to this time?" Although he wasn't sure he wanted to know what the options were.

"First of all, I didn't bring you here, so I cannot 'send' you away, though believe me, I've made inquiries as to how you got here at all. And secondly, when you do leave it will be to a place not of my choosing, nor of yours. Let's just say I hope you like surprises."

But Harry did not like surprises.

Not at all.

Chapter XII

"Dearest Petunia,
I know you must hate me, but I love you and
I miss you. Found work on a road crew for a big
highway here in Coral Springs. As you can see,
the water is blue, like your eyes. Will send money
soon. Kiss the girls for me. Your loving husband,

Rusty Storm"

The postcard arrived two days ago, but it had gotten mixed in with the mailbox fliers of pizza delivery coupons and special discounts on oil changes. But since they could not afford pizza and the car was lucky to be running at all, she hadn't noticed the postcard from Florida until she cleared the kitchen table that morning.

When she was packing lunches for the girls, Corrine was not sure if she should show the postcard to Doris and Aimee, because she was still furious with Rusty for taking off again without telling her, and for leaving them with so little money, and for her being pregnant, and having to accept a second shift at the hospital cafeteria. She worked as a food handler, filling the orders for the patient's trays and sometimes working in the staff dining room, cleaning the tables and making sure the room was neat and orderly for the constant flow of nurses and doctors and aides who came to eat breakfast, lunch, or dinner, or just to get away from the people whose very lives they were responsible for.

"It's almost like having a really big family," she thought, "where everyone has the flu all the time."

She remembered when her boys had been with her and all four of her children and Rusty had been sick at the same time. They lived in a one-bedroom apartment then with the boys in bunk beds on one side of the living room and the girls in one small bed on the other side of their bedroom. Now the boys were in Oklahoma with their grandmother, and she and her daughters were making do in a single with only a shower in the bathroom, and a hot plate in the tiny kitchen, while Rusty was swimming at pristine beaches in Florida and working at another dead-end job so he could maybe send them money to stay exactly where they were.

And yet this was the man she promised to love and cherish, for richer or poorer, in sickness and in health until one of them was in the grave, and love him she did. No matter their financial circumstances, no matter the sacrifices each of them had to make, or even the ones she mostly felt she was making. No matter that he was still the same carefree spirit who just never seemed to find his place in the world, but who kept looking with a boyish sense of adventure and determination, she loved him with all the passion of her heart and her mind. And now with a baby once more stirring inside her, the fruit of her sexual attraction, which in spite of everything they had been through, was stronger and more ardent than the first time they were together under the stars, in the field, on the farm in Oklahoma when she was barely sixteen.

His girls adored him, too, even Doris, who was keenly aware of her father's flaws, and often irritated by her mother's unending patience with him. So, as a surprise, and to keep her family connected in spirit, Corrine put the postcard in their lunch bag. She knew they would want to talk about when Daddy was coming to take them to Florida and ask if they could live near the beach and pick shells like the ones shown in the picture. They would want to tape it to the refrigerator door alongside letters from their brothers, and the other postcards they had gotten from New Mexico and Texas and Louisiana as Rusty made his way east until there was no place else to go except possibly the mythical island of Atlantis.

She waited until the nurse got up from the table. Corrine was glad to see that at least someone had some manners and took the time to clear away their own mess, leaving only a magazine for the next person to enjoy. Usually, it was the aides who cleaned up after themselves. "It's in their nature," she thought. "They're the ones who really keep this place going."

She tried once working as an aide on one of their wards, but she would come home crying every night, telling her husband about how it frightened her to take care of someone who was senile and incontinent and how she simply could not separate heartsick feelings from the tasks she would be expected to perform for them. In the beginning she thought it would be like taking care of a baby. At least that is what they told her when she inquired about the job. "Oh, when they get that old, it's just like taking care of an infant. They won't give you any trouble, and all they ask for is to be kept comfortable," said the woman in Human Resources.

It was hardly that easy, which is why she had such admiration for the aides who did take care of them. She didn't get to know the nurses all that well since she did not work there long. But she knew they were dedicated. Especially Miss Poole, the nurse who had left the medical journal on the table.

So placing the magazine on the chair, she sprayed the tabletop with cleaner, wiped it down, then took the publication with her and placed it in the rack at the back of the cafeteria. It was not something she would be interested in reading, though she did take home older copies of *People Magazine* and sometimes the *Reader's Digest*. She liked to look at pictures of famous people who enjoyed having money and fame and always looked so happy, unless they were going through one of a series of divorces or facelifts or contract disputes. Not that she wanted to be rich, exactly, she just wanted to know her rent was paid, and that the promise of food on the table for her and her children was sound, and that she and Rusty could go to an occasional movie to see these very people up on the screen pretending to be people like them and winning awards for such irony. The other magazine was equally entertaining for the jokes and the stories and the word games she could share with her family.

To be sure, life was seldom fair, but Corrine expected that. She was only hoping for that occasional escape from the woes of a harsh reality which the working poor live through every single day of their lives. "If only we could get to Florida," she thought. "It's cheaper there, and

maybe Rusty and I and the kids could get a fresh start."
But she needed money just to stay one step ahead of the
eviction notice or the red tag from the gas company, or the
disconnect warning from the phone company, and so she
kept working to clean the tables that afternoon, and then
went back to the kitchen to start preparing her share of the
trays for the patients in the East Wing, the ones who, if
they were in their right minds, would refuse the tasteless,
colorless puree she scooped into the sectioned plates,
mush which passed as a semblance of food. Food for
bodies which were past the need for much in the way of
nourishment, but might well be housing minds which
strained at the confines of this mortal coil and would, if
given the slightest chance, fly free over their wheelchairs
and railed beds and all the indignities of growing old and
weak and worthless.

Chapter XIII

Jack arrived at the hospital in record time. He went to the Emergency entrance and asked for Dr. Patterson as the sweet voice on the phone had instructed. He wondered at the time, what with such a nice voice, if her appearance was equally pleasing, but all he heard now was the din one might expect at a major hospital ER and saw only the blurred canvas of activity to match.

He spoke with the obviously overworked resident who still looked like a kid playing make-believe, and who, in grade school probably did play "Doctor" with one of his female classmates much to the shock and dismay of both sets of parents.

"So, you think it was suicide?" he asked him. "I can't imagine Harry was that sad over the news, but you never know about some guys. No matter how tough they seem on the outside, they are really just cream puffs, you know?" Once again, Jack talked too much. Less is more was not an axiom he embraced, but now he regretted giving away information that Harry, whether he lived or died, might not want other people, especially a fellow physician, to know about.

"What was he so despondent about?" asked the Doctor as he made notes in Harry's chart.

"Oh, well, nothing really, he just took a dive on a business deal. Lost a bundle," Jack said. "You know how it is sometimes? Course, you doctors must rake it in, eh?"

"Well, I don't really speculate with my money, Mr. Hollinger, as little as I do make at this point in my career," he sighed. "Nor am I the type to attach so much importance to it that I would do what this man seems to have done, but then, my job is to see he gets the very best care we have to offer here at Madison. Will you see the nurse at the desk and sign the papers to admit him, please?"

"Yeah, sure," said Jack. "Will he come out of it soon, do you think?"

"That's difficult to say. We still don't know what kind and how many pills he took. It appears he wanted very much to die, since we did determine he washed them down with quite a bit of alcohol, but what saved him was the vomiting. You can't take all that on an empty stomach and not expect it to react. I gather he left quite a mess for housekeeping."

"Oh," he said. "Is that what happened? I wondered how he explained what was going on." Jack was trying, without asking outright, if Harry ever regained consciousness. He looked at his watch and decided he could still make it back to the office, take the entire stash of money with him and hop a cab directly to the airport, to hell with the travel agency. Tahiti sounded like the perfect vacation destination. "Just imagine all those thongs on the beach," he thought.

"No, he was never alert enough for any conversation. He babbled a bit, I'm told, but since the housekeeping staff is mostly Spanish-speaking, they weren't much help to the detective."

While Jack was surprised at how grateful he actually was for some "illegal" he would never have the opportunity to meet and thank personally, he didn't let the reference to the police get away. "Ah, so when will I have to talk with the police about this?"

"Here's the card with the detective's phone number. They said if we had any other information, to give them a call, but I think that's something you might want to do in case you can shed any more light on why your friend did it. I'm sure they might want to know about the money, too," said Dr. Patterson, as his pager went off for the second time. So he gave a curt nod and left for the next emergency.

Jack went over to the large counter where the three corridors met. He might have thought about flirting with the nurse who asked for his signature on one of several pages of paperwork, but he was concentrating on how to get out of there quickly and be alone so he could think clearly about what to do next. But when the next burst through the automatic doors was an accident victim who looked very much like he would not be walking anytime soon, since his femur was sticking straight out of his torn and bloody jeans, and his head had been transformed into a swollen, raw, oozing tomato, Jack turned a bit pale and gave the nurse pause as she asked him if he was feeling all right, and perhaps he would like to sit or lie down in one of the curtained areas.

"It might be better if you rested a minute, Mr. Hollinger, or perhaps you should be seen by one of the doctors. May I bring you some water, maybe?" She asked in a soothing, almost cooing tone of voice.

"No, that's okay," said Jack, but he really was feeling awfully light-headed and realized he'd had almost no breakfast and only a swig of bourbon for a late lunch. "Perhaps I should sit for a minute, if you don't mind. I guess hearing about my friend had more of an impact on me than I thought." It was purely a guy thing. He just didn't want her to know he was a complete wimp when it came to real blood and gore. Of course, she knew, having seen macho men react the same way, that this mundane little man was just trying to save face. She walked him over to one of the beds and told him to lie down. She brought him some water and told him to rest until a doctor came by to check him out.

The minute she pulled the curtain closed, Jack took out the flask and finished off the last gulp. He drank the water left for him, and wished he could smoke, but he figured that was probably out of the question. "God Almighty, what a day!" he said, and did a quick review of the events which had brought him to this point. Basically, they all led up to the fact that Harry was alive, and he, Jack, was fucked. Actually, they were both fucked, because Harry was almost alive and Jack, though not having the first clue what do next, was feeling so much like a steaming pile of dog poop that he couldn't do a thing except lie back and wait for the next round of stomach rumba to cease.

With all the stress, and despite the surrounding pandemonium, Jack fell asleep. He dreamed that Harry was leaning over him, looking very much like Riff Raff from *The Rocky Horror Picture Show*, wanting an explanation for why he was not quite dead and why he felt the urgent need to dance "The Time Warp," and where, by the way, was his half a million dollars? Jack was about to get up and put his hands to his hip before taking a step to the right, when he was awakened by the sudden rush of the curtain being swept aside. In walked Dr. Patterson. "Sorry to disturb you, Mr. Hollinger, but the nurse said you seemed a bit under the weather. Perhaps the news was more unsettling than you first thought? Would you like to see Dr. Pickles? Maybe that would help?"

"Gee, Doc," thought Jack to himself. "I can't imagine why seeing the guy I screwed up killing last night would give me anything more than a bad case of the heebie jeebies, but hey, whatever modern medical science prescribes, right? Do you think a bit of Thorazine would help at all?"

"Ah, you mean I can see him? You mean now?" asked Jack.

"Oh, yes, he's up in the East Wing in room 102-B. The nurse will direct you. And thanks again for coming in. Good luck."

"Good luck, bad luck, what the heck's the difference," Jack thought. "If I make it through this freakin' day at all, it'll be like winning the lottery." So he followed the yellow line on the floor as the nurse had instructed and passed through several departments as he made his way to the East Wing. He knew immediately that he was someplace only a stone's throw from the graveyard. It had the smell of old library volumes, musty and stale, though there was the overlying scent of Lysol and other disinfectants, and the occasional Eau de Urine. They had sent Harry to the very place he had been literally, deathly afraid to end up. The area where they cared for the aged patients who were either on line at the pearly gates -- or maybe the express elevator going down to that other place -- all of whom most likely had some form of dementia.

He went right to the room and took in a sharp breath when he saw Harry lying there, breathing deeply with the aid of some sort of tube in his nose and another one in his mouth and various liquid filled ones leading to needles in both his arms. He was in the second bed next to a pale, elderly man who was partially curled up on his side, lying with his mouth open and his eyes closed. For a moment Jack thought the man was dead until he heard him fart long and loud, and smelled what must have been a bowel movement.

"Oh, crap," said Jack and walked out of the room to get a bit of fresh air. The hallway was an obstacle course of linen hampers and wheelchairs and walkers from the more ambulatory residents, all of whom made the cast of *The Golden Girls* look like spring chickens.

"Oh, Jimmy. Jimmy, is that you?" asked one of the women, her eyes beginning to tear up. "I knew you would come. When can we go home? I'm so glad to see you, son." She wheeled over to Jack and squeezed his arm, clutching at his jacket and blubbering, "When are you taking me home?"

Jack was frozen. Suspended in time and space and although his first instinct was to pull her hand away and tell her he was not her stupid son, he wasn't that big of a rat. It would be like kicking a small dog who only wanted to lick your hand. "Well, I, uh, can't really say. Ah, ma'am," he stammered. He was looking around rather desperately, when one of the aides appeared with the grace of an angel, and with a gentle and competent tone and manner, took the woman's hand, immediately re-directing her attention. "Mrs. Keller," said the young Filipina girl in a cheerful and clear voice, just a tad beneath loud, "Your son needs to stay here to talk with one of the nurses. You need to come with me to the Activity Room. You can wait for him there, okay? Come on with me, I will take you." And off they went, the young girl speaking to her as she pushed the older one down the hall.

A few minutes went by and the aide came back. "Oh, Miss," said Jack. "Thank you for your help there. I just want you to know, I'm not her son."

"Yes, of course, I know that," she said, smiling. "Her son comes Sundays, twice a month, if he is not traveling. When I saw you with her, I knew you must be new here. Who are you here to see?"

"Harry Pickles? Attempted suicide? He was brought in this morning?"

"Oh, yes, he is in Room 102-B. That is just around the corner."

"Yes, I've already seen him, actually. Well, just for a minute. Ah, I don't mean to be indelicate, but his roommate is, well, let's just say, he probably needs a change. You know?" Jack leaned in to her, almost whispering.

"Oh," she said nodding. "I'll get someone to take care of him. I am not his aide, but I'll get Rosaria there in a minute. Then you can go in and visit with your friend?" She said, not sure of what the relationship was.

"Yes, Harry was, um, is, a friend. I'm curious why they would put him up here in this ward. You know, he's not that old."

"Well, probably because we have more experience taking care of helpless patients. Don't worry; he is in very good hands here."

"Thank you, I can see that. By the way, what's going to happen with Mrs. Keller? She seemed mighty upset. Will she be expecting to go home?" Jack was not that sure why he asked, but this girl seemed so safe and centered, he just found himself wanting to talk to her. It was actually the first time he didn't have designs on a woman two minutes after they met, though she was certainly attractive enough in a new-bar-of-soap kind of way.

"Oh, she has already forgotten about it. They are like that, you see, their memories betray them. I think they see things through a passing window, as if they were on a train. My grandmother went like that, though we kept her at home with us until she died. People do not do that in this country. You don't have time. You are too busy, so we do it for you," she said.

There was nothing rebuking in her manner. She was just stating a fact. "Yes, that's sad, I guess. I mean it must be harder to grow old these days. Everything is MTV, the Internet and whatnot. You know, instant everything." If fifty was the new forty, Jack still had some wiggle room and didn't think of himself as older. Frankly, he still thought of himself as a fairly together thirty-something, though he didn't look nearly that young at the moment, what with everything he had been through. In fact, what he really thought was that society today is completely masturbatory. People don't want to take the time for romance or courtship, they just want to get the part where they are already smoking a cigarette and contemplating the next sensory injection.

"No one can keep from growing old. Eventually, we all go down that way, you see. What is sad is being helpless. You do not see as well, you cannot walk or feed yourself, maybe, or go use the bathroom alone. That is why we are here. So we can help them with their daily needs and make their last days more comfortable," she said. He was fascinated with how she talked, how melodic her cadence was, each syllable clearly enunciated. Her English was very good. Better, in fact than his.

Jack and the girl, whose name was Nimfa, walked to the room where Harry was ensconced, and found that Rosaria had already been there. She had been kind enough to spray the air with a deodorizer which left the faintest scent of lavender. The man in the second bed had been turned on his other side and there were several pillows cradling him for support.

"After your visit, if you have any questions, please come back to the nurse's station and someone will help you there. I have to take my patients to the dining room and feed them. The dinner trays will be up soon."

"Thank you, Nimfa, for your help," said Jack, and without hesitating, "I hope I see you again."

"Oh, I am here most of the time. I am working two shifts, when they let me, to save up money. I want to go to medical school here in the United States. I was a midwife in my country, and I want to be an Obstetrician. Right now I am studying for the entrance test to the university."

"I can't think of a nicer person to deliver a baby," said Jack, as she turned to walk away, waving ever so slightly and smiling with the broadest, whitest, most giving smile, he had ever experienced.

At that moment, he wanted nothing more than to embrace her, to kiss her, to cherish her and keep her, to champion her every wish and desire, to be her knight in shining armor. Jack had never felt this way before. He was lightheaded again, but this time it was from sheer euphoria. He was already in ARP, acute romantic period, and he didn't even know if she was dating anyone or would be the least bit interested in even having a cup of coffee with him. He had to know.

"Please, Nimfa, before you go," said Jack. "I was wondering if maybe, well, if you would like to have coffee sometime? You know, maybe I could come back later when you have your break, or something?" Jack sounded and felt like a schoolboy asking the new girl out, wondering in that split second if his heart would be broken in a million pieces or float like a feather. His eyes searched her face. She was still smiling.

"Oh, yes," she said. "That would be good. But I cannot meet you tonight; I am studying with a group tonight, but maybe tomorrow? My meal break is at two o'clock. Can you come back tomorrow at two o'clock? I will meet you in the cafeteria. Do you know where that is?"

"I'll find it. I'll be there." Jack promised. He smiled at her and she smiled back and then turned and left.

"I can't believe it," he thought. "With all the shit that has gone on today, there is a silver lining after all." Jack decided he would not swear at all around her. He wanted to wipe the slate clean on all his swearing and drinking and whatever other bad habits he might have. But then there was Harry and the money, and the strange little ad which seemed never to be far from his thoughts. He would have to work these things out tonight. He went to Harry's bedside and told him he was sorry for how badly things had turned out. Jack reminded him that it was not actually his fault that he, Harry, had made this decision, or gotten sick. After all, Jack did complete his end of the bargain. And now there was this young woman, Nimfa, whom Jack told Harry he would never have known except for their mutual circumstances. So in a way, Jack told him, he owed any chance at future happiness to Harry, for throwing up when he did.

There was no reaction at all from Harry. He was in a deep, deep sleep, with only the beeping sound of the heart monitor and the whoosh of the breathing apparatus, and the rhythmic drip of the fluids as his response.

Chapter XIV

"**I** hope you know how incredibly weird this whole thing is, but your ad bugged me so much that when my boyfriend, his name is Roan, by the way, called this morning and told me he couldn't come over, again, I just lost it.

"Well, let's be honest, he's my boyfriend, but he's also someone else's husband and that is what I want to tell you, whoever you are. By the way, who are you?

"I guess, though, if I were that worried about it, I would not have come, but as long as I am here, I'm okay with telling you my story. Please don't use our real names. You said you would keep things confidential. I trust you mean that. Anyway, I met him seven years ago. God, I can't even believe it's been that long. You must think I'm a real sucker, huh?"

And so the story went. It was actually a sad one, not sordid, though there was the element of sex and a bit of kink thrown in for effect, but all in all, a sad story of a young woman caught up in the low tide of love, swept away, and now drowning in a bit of a tidal wave.

The Proprietress would definitely pass this one along to her associates. They needed a lift, as things were becoming more complicated than ever before. First of all, this person, Harry, was an utter pain in her tush, and since he had no right to even be in their company, she felt a decided lack of obligation to share the stories with the likes of him. He lacked both fortitude and finesse and had not a modicum of respect for life, no matter its nature or circumstance. Still, until he left, he would be privy to the stories with the same level of intimacy as the rest of the group.

"Pray that it be soon," she said to herself.

The young boy, however, was a different thing entirely. He really was too young to participate with them. She could not in good conscience share the stories with him. He needed more age appropriate material such as *The Adventures of Tom Sawyer*, or *The Hardy Boys*. Did they still read that type of thing, she wondered? The problem was she didn't know those stories anymore. No one here did. So she would have to improvise, making the best use of the information at hand.

"Once upon a time," she began, as all good stories of childhood should, "there was a man named Harry, and a man named Jack, and they were fast friends. Harry was tall and handsome and charming, and Jack was a toad with a good personality. They lived in a kingdom called Madison, which was very large and full of all sorts of interesting people. One day, Harry found out he was going to become very sick, and so he wanted his friend Jack to make him well."

She made up as much as she could without getting into the exact details of how Harry got to where they were. "When can I go home to Nora?" the boy asked. "Soon, Alfonso, very soon," she said, and had to leave it at that because Nora was not yet ready. She would need to ask for him. She would have to come to The Typing Room and tell her story and make a formal request relative to the disposition of this boy. To plead for his life, if that is what it took to bring him back.

It was not her rule. Even though she was The Proprietress now, she was not the first, but merely one in a long line of women, and some men, who had come before her, and she was only following what had always been, and as far as she knew would always be, the way things were done here in this place, with The Typing Room as their consort and the key to their existence.

When she first qualified to come here, she was angry and disappointed because she had so many plans for her life. She was going to travel, and paint, and perhaps volunteer as a tutor for deaf children, having been a teacher most of her life. She would enjoy her family and her many grandchildren and great-grandchildren and be part of the natural order of things. She was strong-willed and practical, and, other than the occasional expression of anger, was reserved in her expressions of love, except when it came to children. But then only until they developed minds of their own, since the minute they transited to expressing opinions of their own, she distanced herself from them, observing instead how they might turn out, and if the result was to her satisfaction, she would embrace them once more and became a staunch guide and a caring, faithful friend, which is the best any parent can hope to become.

Though she might have been described as the "wire" mother by some of her own, they knew they were loved, and more important, respected as individuals. Oddly, though she did not expect much from them, she always hoped they would be fulfilled in whatever job or life decision they made, and if they were fortunate this would lead them to happiness or something close to it. "True happiness," she always said, "is what you make out of what you have been given. It's a choice you must make. God gives you the canvas and the paint. The rest is up to you."

It was not up to her how the boy went back. He would eventually be returned, but it seemed to The Proprietress that he should be restored to his full life since there was so much of it left. It was different for her and her clan. Theirs was a temporary solution to an untenable situation. Once one of them ultimately made their farewells, another one, sometimes two would shortly follow and the number of them would be restored or increased. At the moment, there were only five, if you counted Harry. There had never been more than twelve, and that was really too many to keep proper track of, even if it meant she would have access to many more stories to share with the group. These individuals were the primary seed for the information on those who would ultimately make the visit, while she was the custodian of The Typing Room, out of which the stories flowered. And although she surmised there were other groups in other places, the means by which they functioned and by what design, she could not say.

How the ads got placed and by what contrivance the money arrived, usually slipped under the typist's door and always by the time they got back home from their visit, were elements she considered to be none of her business. She did not question The Proprietress who passed on the baton and title. She simply understood it and that was all she needed to know. It was the difference between practicing to be a master and simply being one.

The question now was what to do about Harry.

She would like to give this problem the considerable and uninterrupted thought it warranted. If only she did not have to make those annoying appearances, pretending to be awake, eating that intolerable goop they insisted she swallow. She, like the others, did what they had to do especially when their family members came, or when the aides came to tend to them. An eye open, a smile, perhaps, or a truncated wave, like the Queen of England. After all, they were not dead. They were simply somewhere else.

It was not a place which anyone had labeled so far. The Catholics, a religion she herself had been raised in, believed in a place called Purgatory, where it seemed people who were already dead, but not quite acceptable for Heaven, and having been spared from the fires of Hell, languished until they had worked up enough penance points to make it all the way. It seemed you could not earn the points yourself, though. The loved ones you left behind had to recite petitions, or offer Masses for you, or say prayers, with Rosaries counting for quite a number of bonus points. So you had better have been good to your loved ones or there would be no points, and then you'd have to draw from the pool of points that every Catholic sent the way of Purgatory for all the lost souls who had no one to pray for them.

She was not sure about that anymore, but she did know God was real. She wondered when and if she would meet Him. It had been a very long time, years, in fact. But she was content, because at least in the vicinity of The

Typing Room, she was freed from the confines of her corporeal body, and could enjoy the stories she found there.

Plenty of other religions had traveled this way and the occasional agnostic. By the time someone got this far, it was not likely they would still be an atheist, however. Whatever expectation someone might have had, this place was far removed from any of it. To say it was special or even magical belied the enormous relief and utter excitement most of them felt when they first arrived. Initially, most of them thought it was a dream, the kind where you know you are dreaming, but you can't wake up. To some it seemed like just another hallucination, like the ones where they woke up next to a stranger claiming to be a husband or a wife, or the shadow person who was always taking your pocketbook and stealing your money, or moving your car from where you had parked it, forcing you to take the bus or walk a great distance back home. That used to happen to The Proprietress, but she did not remember those things, now she only knew the stories that came from within the four walls of The Typing Room, and that was a state of perfection as far as she was concerned.

There was no time in this place. They existed outside that boundary, too. Thought itself became what was, so she gathered the group together to introduce them to the tale of "Miss Sweets." When it was all over, everyone agreed she would leave that bum and get on with her life.

They offered many suggestions as to how that might be accomplished.

And then, in the spirit of transubstantiation, they voted.

Chapter XV

"What do you mean you're going away this weekend? I thought we were going to get together, you know? Didn't you get my gift, babe?" said Roan, slightly befuddled.

"I told you, I need some time to myself," said Sweetie, fingering the silk teddy and the crotchless panty set he had sent over from Frederick's. "You know I've been working a lot of overtime, mostly on your projects, and I need some time to rest and relax."

"Why don't I come over and bring some champagne and we can 'relax' together. I'll give you one of my famous back rubs," he said in a seductive albeit smarmy kind of way.

She didn't have the heart to tell him they were only famous in his own mind, and in her bed, even as she ached for his touch, her resolve began to weaken. Just then, she heard a beep tone on her phone. The caller ID said "Madison Care."

Hold on a minute," she told him, and then she thought, "I've got a bigger name on the other line."

"Why, what's up?" he asked.

"I have a call coming in," she said, cutting him short. "Hang on."

She clicked over to the incoming caller. "Hello?"

"Yes, this is Mrs. Cramer. I'm calling you from the Madison Care Facility. Is this Ms. Sweets? Ms. Eleanor Sweets?"

"Yes...what do you want?" She was on edge. The only person she knew at Madison was her paternal grandmother, Esther Patricia Sweets, and she had not seen or inquired about her in more than a year. Not since the last time, nearly a year ago, that she was put on Hospice Care for what were the final stages of Alzheimer's.

The Elder Care Advocate could tell this young woman might not want to hear what she had to say, but she was compelled at the request of the next of kin, Walter Sweets and his two sons, Henry and Scott, to tell Sweetie her grandmother was dying.

"I'm calling on behalf of your father and brothers. They're here now at the hospital. Your grandmother is going quickly. If you want to see her before she passes, you should come now. I don't believe, from what Hospice has told me, that she has much time left at all."

There was no response, just the sound of Sweetie breathing. The sound of her welling tears produced no sound at all.

"I...I was just thinking about her earlier today," she managed to say, the lump in her throat growing so large she could barely speak at all. "Are you sure she's terminal, this time?" Sweetie hated to ask, but over the years, she had more than her share of being called to the bedside of this dying woman, only to be caught between the relief of her stabilization and the agony of her continuing illness. It was the fact of her illness and their unwillingness to embrace it for what it was that eventually strained her relationship with her family. They all seemed to believe she would recover, that the insidious disease which ate away at her brain cells would somehow reverse itself and Pat would rejoin the family, once again being the matriarchal presence she had long ago been elevated to given the absence of Sweetie's mother, who had died when she was born.

Walter had taken her into his home temporarily when his wife was experiencing her third and most difficult pregnancy. His daughter was born, and his wife died, and he was grateful and relieved for his mother's kindness and support. She was the familial glue, holding the father and two growing boys and a brand new baby daughter together, and for much of Sweetie's life, her Granny Pat was the source of all her information about how to be a lady. Sweetie was glad that this wise and considerate woman could not possibly have any idea how miserable and ashamed she felt now. She struggled alongside her father with the decision to place Pat in the Madison Care Facility, but its excellent reputation and proximity to her father's home gave them some comfort. The doctors had been very reassuring she would be given first-class care and they saw to it by visiting several times a week.

As time went by (it had been more than five years now,) their visits dwindled down to a once-a-week assembly, but in this they were faithful. Son and grandsons would bring flowers and play tapes for her to listen to and always bring photos, but it was very painful to make the effort when in fact they saw no evidence that she could smell or hear or see the gifts. Still, they kept coming because even if she did not know them, they knew and deeply loved her for the memories of her they kept imbedded in their hearts.

As did many a family member of a person struck down with this illness, they held out an almost pathological desire to see her whole again. They read the literature and met with several experts from the various associations, but no one could give them real hope or assurance. They agreed to try every new medication, even one which was experimental at best. Still, she slowly and steadily declined. She had been on hospice care more than once, and had even outlived four roommates. The nurses, aides and her family dubbed her the "Comeback Queen." Finally it was all too much and Death, who had waited patiently, arrived to escort her on her last journey.

"Ms. Sweets?" asked the caller. "Are you there?"

"Yes, I'm here," she answered.

"Will you come then? I'd like to tell your father if you'll be coming soon," said Mrs. Cramer.

"Yes, tell them I'll be there within the hour," she said finally. "And thank you very much for calling me, Mrs. Cramer." And she hung up the phone.

It rang back almost immediately. She knew it was Roan on the line. She did not want to speak with him. She did not want to share this particular pain with him, and yet she wished he were there to hold her and tell her it would be all right, and make love to her so she could forget how empty and alone she felt at that precise moment. And as the phone continued to ring, she thought back on the last time she saw her Granny Pat and how much this woman had influenced her life.

Pat was born and raised in New York and moved permanently to Madison to be close to her only son and grandchildren after the death of her husband, Walter Sweets, Sr. She was a very active person, keeping busy with any number of projects and helping her son and daughter-in-law, when asked, take care of their young family while keeping herself healthy and fit. The tragedy of her diagnosis was particularly devastating for Walter, Jr., because his young daughter, Sweetie, a difficult child in spite of her nickname, was just leaving the awkwardness of her adolescence and embarking on the serious conquest of adulthood. Both grandparents had been a tremendous help by taking Sweetie to spend summers in their cottage on the Cape.

When her husband died and Granny Pat was alone, she sold the summer cottage, rented out the Manhattan apartment, and moved west to her son's town to organize and hold fast her family, whom she nurtured and protected like any good mother hen with her chicks. Her son and grandsons catered to her every need when she was at home with them, and now they stood by waiting for her last breath.

But where was Sweetie?

Pat hoped her vote in The Typing Room would not go unrewarded.

Chapter XVI

"Will she go, do you think?" he asked. "Maybe there's another way to turn this around. Seems kind of drastic to me."

"It is her time. Death is a personality of great patience, and might be temporarily diverted, but not indefinitely, you know. Besides, it goes both ways, sometimes all we need is permission to take the last few steps," she told him.

"Where will she go...I mean, well, you know?"

"I think her mansion is waiting for her."

"Oh, okay," he said, familiar with the reference to heaven. "That's fine, then, at least it wasn't all for nothing."

"It's never for nothing. Every single thing that happens to each particular person at every minute moment of time is like a fine thread woven on a great loom. Time and space, as we understand it, is the shuttle which passes back and forth, but the design and precisely how our threads look in the overall tapestry is up to a much higher power."

"God, you mean?"

"God, Allah, the Universe, the Force, whatever name makes you feel comfortable. It's all the same. I happen to believe in the personage of God, so I am confident knowing He is in charge of the design."

"Yeah, well, I guess, but if this God is so great, why does he condemn us to a living death? Explain that one."

"You don't listen well, do you?" she said, her own patience wearing thin. "I told you, it's all part of the plan. It's like a single brushstroke in a painting, only the paint does not know if it's on a Jackson Pollock or a Rembrandt. Anyway, what is damnation for one person may be someone else's redemption. Our plight, if you will, gives other people the opportunity to care for us, and to love us with nothing in return. It is almost the only example of unconditional love left in the world. Even babies give something back, but we give nothing back, except the things we can no longer do, or remember, or say, but they remember, and they still love us. Even the aides, the good ones anyway, take care of us not so much because they are paid a king's ransom to, but because it is in their nature to do so. If it is not, they leave and someone else comes who will."

"How does The Typing Room figure into this?"

"You've been here all this time, and still you don't know?" she said, thinking to herself how, if it were possible, she would like to give him a good swift kick.

"I don't mean to be obtuse, but how can the place even exist and nobody knows about it except those who go there?"

"Exactly, it doesn't, except for those who do go there. And we are the beneficiary and eventually so are they. The whole thing is remarkably and exquisitely harmonic, wouldn't you agree? "

"If you say so. Personally, I think we got a raw deal."

"Is that why you tried to take the easy way out?" she said, her tone implying one raised eyebrow.

He said nothing.

Sometimes even Harry was rendered speechless.

Chapter XVII

As she sat by Alfonso's bedside, Nora Poole wondered what kind of a mother she would have been. She had never thought much about her lack of maternal drive. At thirty-five, when most women's biological clocks tick loudly, urging them to move forward towards the decision to start a family, if they hadn't already done so, she had been most satisfied with letting the desire lie there until it got irritated with being ignored and proceeded to find someone else who was more suggestible.

She did not regret any of her decisions. It was not in her character, and besides, she was too old now to even have a child as a single parent, utilizing the many avenues of artificial insemination or even surrogate birth using what in her case must be a dwindled supply of eggs. "A child deserves a mother and a father. A single woman is often viewed as only half a family," she thought. Still, she pictured what life would be like with Alfonso as her son. She knew there was no hope of ever marrying, and she did not need nor want the company of a man in her life. She was a maiden lady and would remain so unto death.

It was getting late in the day. Her other patients were getting their evening meal, and she had filled the feeding device for Alfonso and checked on the antibiotics he was now taking in. His fever was held down, but still above normal. If by morning it did not respond more favorably, the doctor might be forced to consider a surgical means to determine its cause.

Nora thought about the woman who had given birth to this boy, and wondered to the point of tears how anyone could have been reduced to such a low state as to try and murder a child. She knew from the records that his mother had been a drug addict and an alcoholic, but was clean and somewhat sober during most of her pregnancy, only to take up with the pipe and the bottle soon after his birth. He'd had a series of "uncles," none of whom were abusive, thank God, but all of whom were neglectful, seeking only the thrill of the hunt for a high, and taking off when parenthood interfered with having a good time.

Alfonso had been on the radar with the Department of Social Services since he was born. The state had been a more consistent guardian than any fleeting family member, and his future was in their hands. Being their ward, they could decide at any given moment to send him to another hospital, one less costly than Madison, or to a state run home. They had been informed of his worsening condition and with the prospect of surgery and more intense, and therefore, more expensive care, it was entirely possible that this poor and desperately ill orphan would not rank very highly on any bureaucrat's list of the best way to spend allocated funds, especially when the return would be so negligible to anyone who did not love him.

"I love you, dearie," she whispered to him, and then she whispered again as if he were responding, "I love you, too."

There was nothing more she could do for him tonight. It was getting late and she would need her rest in preparation for any battles that might rage tomorrow. She planned to go straight home and get a good night's sleep, and return to the hospital bright and early the next morning. She spoke to the relief nurse and gave very specific instructions about calling her if there were even the most negligible changes.

Nora was just about to leave the hospital when she ran into one of the aides from the East Wing. Nimfa, she was pleased to say, had been one of her team members, and was by far one of the most caring and conscientious persons she had ever known. She would make a fine doctor some day, as Nora was the one who encouraged her to continue with her education. They spoke and Nimfa related the sad news that Mrs. Sweets had died. They consoled each other over the news, and Nimfa described how it was rumored the woman was completely alert and even spoke when her granddaughter showed up, having been called to her side with the news of her impending death.

It never ceased to impress on them how prescribed the process of dying is. First the body would get noticeably cooler to the touch, starting with the extremities. Most of the older patients needed extra blankets and there were always an abundance of crocheted and knitted coverlets supplied by a local church group or charity organization. They would spend much more of their time sleeping. Both Nora and Nimfa were well aware of the difference between sleep and a person simply wanting to shut out the world. Incontinence and disorientation were common in Alzheimer's sufferers, but this was also a sign in patients dying from some other illness. Breathing patterns would change, and they would become decidedly restless, pulling at their nightshirts, or the bed linens. Their urine would reduce and become dark, like strong tea. Most dementia patients would lose the ability to chew or swallow food, so if the family had not signed a Do Not Resuscitate order, or the person had left no clear instructions about how to deal with this problem, they would be fed through a tube. Nimfa and Nora knew that for this type of patient, it only prolonged the inevitable, and it seemed to them to be a cruel artificial extension to the race when one was almost at the finish line.

What did surprise them was that this woman was surrounded by her family at the moment of her passing. In their experience, most old people died alone. The family members would come and sit and wait, sometimes for days on end, taking turns to be sure their loved one was not alone, and just when they took a moment to get some coffee, or get up to use the restroom, or take a short walk to stretch their legs, when they returned, the person had taken the opportunity to expire. Death is a very private thing, they decided.

Nimfa told Nora about the new patient, Dr. Pickles, and how she had also met a friend of his who seemed like he might be interested in her, and that in turn, she was attracted to him. Nora cautioned her not to let anyone, certainly not any man, keep her from her studies. "Men want to be the center of your life, they don't like taking second place to anyone or anything," Nora said. Still, she thought, if only I had not been so rigid in my thinking, I might have married and had children, a son perhaps.

They gave each other a quick hug and Nimfa, weighed down with her books, went off to her study group, and Nora exited the building and walked to the bus stop.

Chapter XVIII

Jack was a bit taken aback when he entered The Typing Room. Initially, he felt it had the same off-putting decorum shared with the Savings and Loan. The elegant furnishings, a bit too refined for someone of his upbringing and decided lack of taste. But it was pristine, and the high ceiling and sparse furnishings saved him from feeling penned in, as it was not that large a room. He was particularly impressed with the buttery softness of the wall covering's material, which begged to be touched, and so he did.

He was not the least bit concerned or confused by the fact that no one was in the room when he arrived. He assumed for the moment that someone would know he was there and they would present themselves in a timely manner. In fact, he had no concerns at all about being physically overwhelmed in any way. Very few people had ever gotten the best of him in a fight, having learned early in life to defend himself by whatever means necessary, including some moves not listed in the Marquis of Queensbury rule book, so he was content to stand there and wait.

The slim table near the window was amusing to him in that it had an old Brother typewriter, like the one he had had in his college dorm room. This one, he could see, was exactly like the ones in the school library that required one quarter per half hour of time to use. He had spent many nights there typing term papers until he had saved enough to get one of his own. The money had come from his first and most awful job of cold-calling people to find out if they wanted time shares at a resort in Mexico he was sure did not even exist. Still it was work, and it paid for his books and his Saturday night poker games, where he made more money and eventually most of his money as he expanded his talents to include a floating crap table and small numbers racket. It was not until the local Mafioso type took an interest and convinced him it was best to leave such gaming activities to the professionals, rather than risk a broken kneecap or two. But because in those days he looked like he could snap a leg or an arm with ease, they did offer him a job, which he respectfully and successfully declined, knees intact.

After his confessional visit with Harry and hoping against hope he would have but a slender chance with the lovely Nimfa, Jack went back to his office to retrieve the ad. Although the office was closed, he knew it would still be in the trash can because the cleaning crew would not arrive for another hour. Getting the night guard, Sgt. Fred Boonnark, to open the door was no problem. Good ol' Freddy liked cigars and Jack had plied him with a Cuban now and again, so when he left, Jack gave him one from his own stash, which he kept in a locked file drawer in his desk. Special, high balance customers were always grateful for the gift, and so he knew the guard would turn a blind eye to this nocturnal visit.

When he arrived at the address on Kenmore Road, he looked over to the park across the street where earlier he had decided, wisely after all, against making the call to the hotel about Harry and the smell. It was empty, but softly lit by vintage lampposts which gave a soft, sensuous glow in the night air, rather than those all revealing, harsh spotlights that did little to invite an evening walk or a romantic encounter on a park bench.

The walk up the four flights did not wind him in the slightest bit, because he was still in pretty good shape, being a regular at the spin class. He knocked, as everyone did the first time they came, and then opened the door, without waiting for a response.

Having assessed his surroundings, from the vantage point near the door, he stepped closer to the desk. From behind the desk chair, he blinked deliberately and scowled and pursed his lips when he saw the stately crème-colored envelope that bore his name in textbook penmanship. Though he had doubts about the delicate chair's ability to hold him, he sat down and tore it open and began to read.

> *Dear Mr. Hollinger,*
>
> *We wish to thank you for coming here tonight. We have been anticipating and preparing for your arrival with a flurry of activity. First of all, please do not be the least bit concerned about the chair you sit in. It is handcrafted from the finest mahogany by a reputable New England woodworking establishment. It will bear most any weight with ease.*
>
> *Secondly, be comforted in that we hold no judgment of the slightest nature regarding your activities of the past forty-eight hours. What's done is done. After all what matters most is what a person will do, not what they have done. To that end, we*

know you will have quite a tale to share with us. One filled with remorse to be sure, but also full of optimism for what will undoubtedly be a rather drastic change of lifestyle and a renewing of your mindset.

Please take a moment to notice the quarters in the dish next to the typewriter. We understand you are familiar with the need for these. We ask that when you are finished typing you place the papers in the basket. Do not bother to correct any typographical errors; we are more interested in the content of your story than the execution of same.

Please use the pen, not the pencil, thank you, to sign your name at the end of the last page. And please write in the code from the ad which brought you to us. If you would be so kind as to also, please, turn off the lamp just before you leave.

When you return to your office tomorrow morning, please check your box for the appropriate compensation. When you do, you will have the peace of mind you seek. The rest will come in due time.

Thank you again for your visit, Mr. Hollinger. If you find satisfaction with the arrangement, you are welcome to return anytime.

Sincerely,

The Typing Room

Jack typed well into the wee hours of the morning. In fact, when he was getting ready to leave, light was beginning to pour through the window; so much so, he almost forgot to turn off the lamp because the room took on a light of its own. He signed the last page and was dutiful in printing the code from the ad. He was relieved the rainwater stains had not obscured the numbers and the letters which he was required to pen under his signature. He didn't think he would ever come back, no matter what the letter in his pocket said. Like someone who is newly baptized, he was sure he would never sin again.

In another part of the city, at The Madison Hospital and Care Facility, in room number 102, in the bed near the window, a tear fell from Harry's right eye.

Another one fell from Jack's left one as he walked slowly down the stairs.

Chapter XIX

"**M**ama, will Daddy be coming home soon?" asked Aimee, as her mother tucked her in. Corrine looked over at her other daughter, Doris, and saw she was sound asleep, her breathing deep and regular, her raven hair glossy and thick, cascading down her back. She would probably go salt and pepper in her later years, just as her father had when he turned thirty, and his father before him and even his granddad when he reached his dotage. She was quite the beauty with her black hair and auburn eyes, and a fresh, fair-skinned face with the most delicate spray of freckles across the bridge of her perfect nose. Looking at her reminded Corrine of how much she missed her husband, Rusty, because she was the one child who looked most like him. Aimee, on the other hand, was blonde and had the ruddy complexion and deep blue eyes her brothers and mother shared. Doris would do great things in life, her father always told her. Corrine ached in her heart that so far this intelligent and gifted child's greatest accomplishment was being an unpaid *au pair* to her younger sister because "Mama" was too busy working two jobs to keep the wolves away from the front door. "Damn you, Rusty!" she thought.

"Well, of course he will be, honey. You know he couldn't be without his girls for long. Now, it's time you got some dream time. The sun will be up before you know it, and you don't want to be all sleepy eyed when it does."

"I won't be, Mama, but I would sleep better if you sing to me."

"Well, I would but I don't want to wake up your sister, baby. See how peaceful she is, you wouldn't want me to disturb her." Corrine said, brushing aside Aimee's bangs. Her hair was just beginning to grow out from a rather dreadful haircut she gave herself one day. Her hair looked like it had been gone over with a pair of sheep shears, but Aimee was such an easygoing kid she didn't mind a bit. Doris, however, was mortified to be seen with her sibling, who, as she put it, looked like she escaped from what Doris called the "looney tunes bin."

"Oh, Mama, she won't wake up," cooed Aimee. "She can sleep through anything. Please, Mama, sing?"

"Okay," said Corrine, sitting down on the floor near the edge of the small bed, next to her young daughter's head. "What song do you want to hear?"

"The sunshine song," she said. It was always the same tune.

"You are my sunshine, my only sunshine. You make me happy when skies are grey. You'll never know dear, how much I love you. Please don't take my sunshine away." Corrine sang this tune because it was the only one she remembered from her own childhood when her grandmother would sing it to her as they sat together on the front porch of their farmhouse, rocking back and forth as the sun sank down into the field of amber waves. Before she got to the last lyric, Aimee was sound asleep.

Corrine touched the top of each daughter's head. When she crawled into her own bed, she held a pillow close to her chest and hoped the sound of her tears would not wake up the sleeping children. Florida might as well be on the moon for as much chance as she thought they had of getting there anytime soon. And there was no telling what Rusty was up to. Not that she didn't have absolute faith in him. The funny thing is, she did. Because he was deeply in love with her and they both knew it. A man like Rusty will do almost anything for the woman he loves. "Except grow up." she thought and drifted off to sleep. She dreamed about lying nude on a beach with sand as white as snow and as soft as baby powder. The warm water was turquoise blue and clear right down to the sandy bottom, which was strewn with shells of every size and shape. She was holding on to her husband's hand and she could feel the spray from the waves as she ventured in deeper and deeper into the surf until the water turned a bottomless cerulean. But she felt safe in the deep water because he was swimming around her like a playful dolphin, and she was very, very happy at last and willed herself not to wake for the rest of the night, but to continue dreaming until dawn.

Chapter XX

"What if this is all just a dream?" Harry asked The Proprietress. "What if I'm dreaming you and this place and these people, you know like on TV when the writers poop out and can't come up with anything more credible."

"Oh, as if television was so true to life. Even the reality shows are fixed, did you not suspect even that?"

"Are you saying this because you 'know,' or are you just guessing?"

"I never 'guess.' If I do not know something, I keep my mouth shut about it. Something you should consider if you wish to stay here." She could not help putting him in his place, because verbal sparring with him had become an amusement, even at her age, and the fact remained he was less wearisome now than when he first came, and did add a bit of spark in a situation which was beginning to be more difficult to control, even for The Proprietress. It made her wonder if she would be leaving soon. She had been here a long time. No one stayed forever. The Typing Room was simply not designed that way. Those who traveled this far were always closer to death than anybody ever realized.

"All I am saying is this is no dream. Sometimes, we do dream, but not like this. If we have come here, there is no need to dream anymore, because the stories we find in The

Typing Room take the place of dreams. Besides, how can a brain which is dying dream anything substantive? And for that matter, you are not dying yet in the same way all of us are now. You might recover, at least for a while. And if you do, you will think you did dream, and that is how you will remember us and this place, and in time all of it will fade away, the way dreams are supposed to."

"So you think I will go back?" He had been afraid to ask too many questions about this, fearing the worst. Though what might be worse than dying now was the very thing which brought him to this point, that and Jack's untimely fumble of it all. "And what will happen to me if I do? Will I still go batty and end up here anyway?"

She was annoyed with his use of the term "batty." It was highly inappropriate, but she remained composed. "I cannot say. It isn't my plan, remember? I can only manage what I am responsible for and you being here is a situation none of us quite expected. My primary concern for the moment is the boy. He is the random factor here. I cannot recall a time when anyone came who was not ill the way we are, or in your case, will be."

"I thought you knew everything?" he said, in a challenging tone.

"Let's just say, I know more than you, though how difficult that would be under any circumstance is a factor which is negligible at best."

"Are you calling me stupid? I am...was, a doctor for Christ's sake. I used to treat old biddies like you!" Harry was fuming, and he lost all sense of where he was and with whom he was dealing.

"I see, well, you certainly won't be plying your trade any time soon, will you? It is educated fools like you with no common sense who pervert the medical profession. May God help anyone who had the misfortune to be your patient! And while we are on the subject, is it not in your sworn oath to 'do no harm'? What about that? Should that not apply to you first and foremost? Maybe the phrase *'physician, heal thyself'* is something you should have pondered a bit more carefully instead of being such a scared little weasel. But forgive me on behalf of everyone here, I feel quite fortunate your friend Jack is such a bumbling fool. After all, he has brought us one of the best stories I've heard in nearly a decade and he would not have, were it not for the deal you and he made in that bar. Two conspirators, indeed. Ha! Two ninnies are more like it. How dare you take the easy way out! Do you know what we all went through to get to this place? Have you any idea the indignities we have suffered and the pain and torment our families have endured for all the memories they have of us which we can no longer share with them? The desperate loss they feel and the anger and fear of oftentimes being the sole caretaker with little or no respite? Do you? Of course you don't. I don't even know why I brought it up. As if you would have the slightest notion of what it means to make any kind of focused effort for anyone or anything that did not serve the glorious and perfect you!"

She hadn't been this angry since the mugging, and somehow it felt kind of good to let off some steam. Harry, on the other hand, was glad she could not physically get to him. He had the feeling she would have scratched his eyes out before he could muster a defense. And yet, there was something to be said for having an intellectual battle, in keeping with the situation and all. She was older to be sure, but there was still an excitement in a verbal repartee with a woman who was clearly his intellectual superior, even if he would never, ever admit it.

Before all this happened, Harry really was quite the *bon vivant* and was well-read and well-traveled and had a distinct taste for the finer things in life. He had an appreciation for fine art and classic literature, and he loved music, especially jazz; Coltrane among his favorites, as was the lovely Billy. He had married once, just long enough to graduate from medical school and the ensuing years of internship and residency. But he couldn't keep his hand out of the cookie jar, so to speak, and had numerous dalliances with nurses and even some patients. His bride was an older, cosmopolitan woman who, when he became more of an embarrassment than an amusement, departed for Paris, leaving him a tidy settlement in the form of paid-off student loans. He vowed never to marry again, and with the money he was no longer in debt over, he could begin a practice sooner than most and set up shop in Beverly Hills along with two other plastic surgeons, all promising the fountain of youth to anyone willing to put up with the pain of transfiguration.

He first met Jack when he brought wife number-one in for a boob job. Not that she wasn't a perfectly figured woman, mind you; just a tad boyish in the bosom, but with a splendid rear end, and Jack had wanted the front and the back to match. They were not yet friends until he returned a couple of years later with wife number-two, who was actually quite the contortionist, it turned out, and was just in for a much needed rhinoplasty, since her honker was as outstanding as her chest. What clearly fascinated Harry was how this guy could get any woman much less two pretty decent fillies. So while wife number-two was recovering in the nearby hotel suite, which he and his partners acquired as part of their splendid first-class service, Harry invited Jack out for a drink. And so their friendship began, because Harry liked the fact that Jack was actually a man's man. Not some uppity-puppety 90210 bore who wanted their underage mistress to have tits the size of Pamela Anderson, Jack was just an otherwise unremarkable guy who liked to drink and smoke and bullshit the way men do when they are together.

He didn't know beef from bull's foot about what was happening in the world of art or music, but he could quote the stats on almost any sport and knew a fine cigar from a poor one and how to get them. He was a bit on the chatty side, but he always had an entertaining joke or off-color story to share. He was not vain about himself, but wanted the women he squired to be knockouts, and they were, even if they needed a little more help than Mother Nature had initially provided.

In every way he was Harry's opposite and that made for a splendid friendship. One which served Harry well, up to the point where he awoke in the hotel room and saw the horrified look on the maid's face screaming in what he assumed was Spanish, as he blurted out "I'm going to kill that son of a bitch!" just before going blank. It seemed only the briefest of moments before he woke up to find himself in the company of several rather elderly personalities, all led by The Proprietress who was reading a letter to them from some woman whose husband had left her with two young daughters.

"I'm sorry," he said finally. "I shouldn't have overreacted. I hope you don't really think I am stupid, because really I'm not about most things, but you do have a point. I should have handled this whole thing better. It's just that I am scared and I don't like not being in control. I suppose that fear above all is what drove me to do what I did."

She thought for a moment before responding. She had felt the same way. It was a terrible and desolate time for her when she was first diagnosed. They told her she was in the early stages, where she could still live alone with some supervision, but that very soon she would progress to the more degenerative level, requiring confinement and almost constant care. She tried to comprehend, but how does one really process such devastating and paralyzing news that soon you would be rendered almost invisible to your friends and family and ultimately even to yourself? She tried to read up on it, but found the more she learned, the worse she felt. She did take some comfort in knowing the president she voted for had it, and that so did several celebrities, and because of their illness, funding was freer-flowing to research studies and the like. But it would be a long time in coming, too long to help her.

And so she handled this most unpleasant state of affairs the way she lived all of her life, with careful planning, and trust that her family would take care of her as long as they could. Still she was not the least bit pleased when the time did come much sooner in fact than anyone realized it might, for her to be placed in a more secure environment. She was driven there under the falsest of circumstances and left. She still had enough of her capacities, though not many, to curse her son and daughters for their betrayal. Her son, in particular, did not get over being the recipient of such verbal venom and for years refused to visit. He wanted to remember her as she was. There was no shame in this, and The Proprietress wished she could let him know she held no grudge. After all, he had been a good and thoughtful caretaker for the many years after she became widowed, but his own health was in question and he had a family to raise and a life to live.

As he withdrew, the other children came to the forefront and each handled what share of the burden they could, one daughter handling all the financial matters, and another, who lived quite a distance away, all the emotional ones, with the one who lived nearby taking on the task of almost daily and then weekly and then monthly visits as her deterioration took its toll on son, daughters, grandchildren and great-grandchildren, each in their own way.

The first few weeks were the hardest for her and the staff, whom she erroneously suspected were drugging her food. But in time she did adapt and in spite of the fact that this place was designed and built specifically for men and women with this same desperate condition, she managed to escape once and won the unofficial award for being one of only three who had ever accomplished what her family had been assured was impossible. The other two were men and they had scaled the wall. It was simply that she observed over a period of time when the deliveries came in and out of the back gate, and merely walked out when their backs were turned. She wandered down the street, where she came upon a school where the children were in recess. Thinking perhaps she was back at one of the schools where she herself had been a teacher in charge of the yard twice a week, she stayed to watch over her students until a car drove up with one of the aides who asked her if she wanted some lunch and a ride in the car. Being hungry, she obliged. She was somewhat pleased with herself when she returned to the day room and felt a clear sense of pride, if only fleeting, that she had managed to outwit them.

"I understand, and I know what you mean. It is too horrible to talk about, so let's not, for now. Let's just be glad we are here," she told him. "I do have one question. You do know what will happen to your money, don't you? After all, it's not like you will need it, so I hope the plans meet with your approval."

"Sure," he said. "I figured that one out. Whatever it takes to make up for being such a fool is more than okay with me."

"So you are a bright fellow after all," she said as if winking. "I thought as much."

Harry appreciated the praise, coming from one so wise. Besides, she held all the aces in this game.

Chapter XXI

Alfonso's condition was worse. His fever was elevated because the antibiotics, strong as they were, proved helpless against what the doctors now surmised might be a complete decline of one or both kidneys. He was headed for renal failure and this posed the real likelihood he would be yanked from Madison and put in a less costly establishment, that is to say a county-run facility, while they debated the probability of locating a kidney for transplant. Even if they found one, in an irreversible coma, he was an unlikely candidate on whom to waste a perfectly good organ that some other person would better benefit from.

Nora had arrived extra early that morning, and went straight to his room, reading all the updates to the chart and overlapping her schedule with the night nurse in order to get firsthand all the nuances of his care and subsequent responses throughout the night. The night nurse was as gentle with the information as she could be, but she also knew Nurse Poole was a highly trained expert and could absorb and process even the most mundane bit of information, so she had made notes of her own, knowing what a personal interest this nurse was taking in the little boy. That in itself might demonstrate to the administration a lack of professionalism, but this particular nurse was a mother and recognized the devotion

Nurse Poole showed as being akin to how she cherished her own children. Nora thanked her and only then did she punch her time clock to begin her shift.

"Good morning, Alfonso. How's my boy today?" Nora said cheerily as she cupped her hand on his forehead and on his cheek. She checked on his urine collection bag and saw that the color of what little specimen there was resembled a strong brew of Lipton. His face and body were warm and clammy. She combed his hair and wiped his face with a cool washcloth. For a nanosecond she thought she saw what might be a tear. She took in a sharp breath and gasped before she realized it was a drop of water from the washcloth. Regaining her composure, but feeling the weight of a heart bound and nearly broken, she touched the droplet and then her lips. "I love you, dearie," she softly said to him. "More than you'll ever know."

What she could not know even in her dreams was that Alfonso did know, and that it might appear to her, were she so privileged to transcend time and space and every unknown place between life and lifelessness, that he and The Proprietress stood side by side in the company of The Typing Room, his head leaning inward as he clung to her with her arm around his shoulder in quiet consolation.

"I love you too, Nora," he told her. "When are you coming to take me home?" And turning to The Proprietress, he asked, "When will she come to get me?"

"Soon, I am sure, child, very soon." She told him, but was really not at all sure about anything now.

Chapter XXII

It all began strangely with a dream she'd had one night after her daytime aide came into her room and said goodbye. Her evening aide was equally conscientious about coming in to say hello. The Proprietress thought it was so very kind and good of them to continue talking to her as if she could hear them. Notwithstanding her pronounced deafness, her eyesight had gone from bad to worse over the years and her eyeglasses, for all the good they did, were impractical for someone who was almost always lying on their side, or appearing to be sleeping, or was in fact, not conscious in the worldly sense of the word, and so any skill she had at reading lips was long gone. Still, she appreciated it and felt they must have had good home training to treat the ill and elderly so well.

She felt sure it had been a dream and not one of those near-death experiences she used to see on the programs about psychic phenomena or other such hocus pocus. She knew she had not died because when she woke up everything was the same. And the daytime aide didn't treat her any differently than she had the day before, always the same smile and cheery voice. Nothing to indicate there had been a medical problem of any kind. They saw that she was awake and alert, to the extent that she was, and this pleased them so much, The Proprietress had been quick to see right from the start that this was a good way to get them to tend to her more often. When one is a baby, there is a definite survival instinct which translates to looking cute and cuddly and crying on cue for food or warmth or a clean diaper. When one is like she was, it paid to be alert, at least some of the time and certainly during the morning meal. That assured fresh clothes and a clean bed and hot food, though it could hardly be called that, much as she was sure the kitchen tried to make it appealing in both taste and texture.

Before she arrived at The Typing Room, she'd forgotten about how wonderful it was to eat a number-one combination at her favorite Mexican restaurant, or to have a glass of Cabernet, or to indulge in the pure delight of chocolate-chip cookies fresh from the oven. Not her oven to be sure; she'd always been a rather dreadful cook, so much so that when her dear late husband asked what was for dinner, he used to say "what shall we open tonight," referring to her predilection for canned foods of every variety. He made up for it all by becoming a rather inventive chef, and never ceased to amaze with what he could cook on the outdoor grill.

That was the saddest part, if there was just one, about the condition she was in. When she was in her bed, she did not remember all the years they had spent together, and when she was in The Typing Room, she did. Sometimes she dreamed about him, but even her dreams were ephemeral, shadowy realms which did little to make sleeping any better than being awake. Except for the one dream which prompted her to leave on a journey, which ultimately brought her to The Proprietress she would ultimately replace in The Typing Room.

"What are you thinking about?" Harry asked her. He was feeling rather bored and wondered if she might have a new story to tell.

As if sighing, she said to him, "Nothing really, I was just remembering a dream I had." And to quell any untoward remark and begin another verbal dual, she added, "A real dream, Harry, not this place."

"I seem to dream quite a bit, myself. I guess that is why I was wondering about it the last time we talked."

"No, this was a true and straightforward dream. As real as any I ever had, so real in fact I thought I had died and gone to heaven."

"Really, what was the dream about?" asked Harry.

She would have given him such a look, and perhaps a wry smile. "Have you been rendered deaf somehow? I think I just said, I died and went to heaven. Well, not to heaven, but almost. Most of the way, I'm sure. And no, to answer any question you might have on the subject. I did not have one of those afterlife things. I'm still here, and so are you, and I am not entirely persuaded those types of things really happen at all, because if it is anything like my dream, not one single person alive today would ever come back. Not ever."

"Must have been some dream. Do you feel like talking about it? Maybe share it with us like one of the stories? Jack's story, by the way, was a real hoot! I just hope he gets the girl in the end, you should pardon the expression...I mean, well, you know what I mean."

"Yes," she said as a matter of fact and with no glint of humor, "I do. But the dream is not a story and cannot be shared with the others." She hesitated. He took the bait.

117

"Well, perhaps you can tell me? I'd love to hear it, seeing as how I may have blown any chance at all getting there myself."

"I would like to tell someone, Harry, so it might as well be you given the parameters of this situation. Perhaps there is hope for you still, seeing as how you are not dead and are willing to make amends for your rather reckless decision."

"It was not like my other dreams. This one was remarkable. As if I were seeing a movie where the screen wraps around you and the speaker system surrounds you with crystal clarity. I could feel myself falling down a long narrow cave-like structure. I was falling but at the same time I was floating down, almost as though my flight was controlled so as not to frighten me with the helplessness one might imagine having after taking a step off a high cliff. I was not as old as I am now; I seemed to be younger and stronger, more like my "prime," if you will. The cave turned in such a way that I found myself moving within a long, high-ceiling corridor. On the walls and all along the arches there were shards of broken mirror. And in each of the reflections I could see and hear each and every event of my life, from the most public to the most intimate. As I passed I caught glimpses of the joy and sadness I had both experienced in my own life and that which I caused either by my actions or my failure to act. I saw the consequences of each deed I performed and each word I spoke and even the very thoughts in my mind. I could see how a single gesture had a ripple effect (which I was at once impressed and horrified to know in that moment as I passed the glass,) had an impact on people I had not met or known, or would not know no matter how long I lived. A terrible, aching grief came over me. It was so sad, Harry, so appallingly, terrifyingly, frighteningly sad, that I did not think I could go on. I wanted to disappear out of shame for all the loathsome and cruel things I had done, even though at the time, they did not seem all that bad.

"And then, Harry, and this is why I am sure, in spite of what you did, you will be forgiven and go to heaven, I think I met Jesus. Now I know you don't believe in Him or maybe you are not really sure about God in general, but I tell you, I met Him in this dream. And for the first time I knew what it was to be loved. At first there was a glow of white light, which seemed to come from the glass pieces. What was shadowed mirror became blinding brilliance and the radiance that emanated from the splintered sections surrounded me and pierced me and I was overcome by it and enveloped by it. I was not me anymore at all. I was absorbed into this illumination and became a part of it, though any line of distinction between it and me was not perceptible. And yet I finally knew exactly what the words 'I am' mean and what my place in the world and in the very universe actually was. I cannot describe it to you in words. There are no words I have ever read or written or spoken which can give you a respectable conception of it. Then, the light took on a personality, for lack of a better way to describe it to you. And I heard a voice, a marvelous, mellifluous voice, asking me 'Well, what do you think?', and I went from the depths of hell, which I could only guess was anything this entity was not, to an ecstasy I did not want to ever be without. I could only say how sorry I was for being outside what I was now dissolved into and a part of, and I knew what it was to be known in body and mind and at last my soul. I asked if he was Jesus, because certain as I was about being dead at that moment, I knew this was the quintessential love with a capital 'L' I had been taught about in Sunday school and been preached to from the pulpit, and there was no doubt this was the Lord come to take me into paradise. I wanted to stay. There was nothing which could have persuaded me to return to my previous life, and I was beyond sorrow to know I could not stay because somehow it had been made clear to me it was not my time yet to die. I would return again someday through this hallway, but would never have to make the journey back. When I woke up, I was sobbing uncontrollably and wailing so that the aides and the nurses both thought I was going to go into cardiac arrest and wondered if they should ignore the DNR note pasted to the top of my bed.

"And that is my dream, Harry."

Harry did not say anything. He would have hugged her if he could, or if she would allow it, which he felt was probably out of the question. So instead he just stayed with her until time passed and he and she returned to the world outside The Typing Room.

Chapter XXIII

"**W**ould you prefer a rosewood finish or this lovely champagne brushed metallic? The rosewood has a really remarkable depth, but the metal is becoming a fast favorite. Very up-to-the-minute, don't you agree? Both come with either a satin or a silk lining. I think the silk is especially wonderful, don't you? Feel how luxurious this is. We have a wide variety of color, or if you prefer something custom dyed, we can do that as well." The funeral director was a peppy young woman who had all the makings of another "Vanna," or one of those auto show display girls, the kind who draws your attention to the new fender design or the craftsman quality of the dash with an artful sweep of both hands. It is a job only few should want to have, but since death is a very dependable business to be part of, it offers a reliable and lucrative career choice if one is so inclined and not adverse to the smell of formaldehyde.

"I think the rosewood with the silk would be nice, don't you, Sweetie?" asked her father, Walter Sweets. "And peach for the color. She had a favorite blouse in peach."

"Well, sir, if you bring the blouse over tomorrow, we can match the color precisely, for only a nominal charge."

Sweetie, her nose red and stuffy, could only nod; her eyes puffy, aching from crying so much. She had made it to the East wing at Madison in time to see her Granny Pat one last time before she died. When she got there the hospice worker told her not to be too disappointed if her grandmother did not wake up. She was really at death's threshold, she was told, and now that her granddaughter was there, she could go at any moment. "Sometimes they wait for that one last person before they surrender," she said to Sweetie.

Pat had her own room, unlike most of the residents on the floor. She was a private pay patient, so her son had elected to spend the money for a larger, single room, complete with a small sitting area near the bed. Since the son and grandsons came on a regular basis, there was a TV on one of her antique dressers and two comfortable armchairs in a soft chocolate mohair fabric in addition to the metal and plastic guest chairs supplied by the hospital. Her bedding was also her own, beautiful hand sewn quilts which Pat used to joke privately to her granddaughter were made at her "bitch and stitch" bees with all the ladies she met with on the Wednesdays their husbands would meet and discuss politics and smoke cigars and play poker.

There was a large armoire in the corner of the room which held six quilts, several sets of pure smooth cotton sheets and two goose-down pillows with embroidered shams. Hung on the rod were thirteen nightshirts, all white, with different colored piping on each gown. There were two silk quilted bed jackets, one teal blue and one peach, both a gift from Sweetie. A florist came once a week and delivered a fresh bouquet of seasonal flowers. Pat used to say she loved informal displays that looked as if someone had simply gathered a handful of a garden's offerings and plunked them in a glass jelly jar. Even though they were in the middle of the Alzheimer's ward at Madison, this room was a welcoming oasis.

Sweetie hugged her father and her brothers and let them know they could take a break if they wanted to, since she would not leave her grandmother's side. They'd been there for a while and had said their goodbyes, so they felt comfortable in leaving for a moment. They knew Sweetie had not been there in several months, and understood she might want to say goodbye in private. Sweetie pulled up a chair to the head of the bed. Her grandmother looked younger to her somehow, the lines in her face had smoothed out a bit and her hair, which was silvery white, had been braided and lay across her shoulder with feathery tendrils framing her face. She is what is called a handsome woman, with strong, direct features, bordering on the androgynous, almost angel-like.

"I'm here, Granny," she said, taking hold of her hand, kissing it and holding it to her face, her tears washing over both women's fingers, Sweetie's skin bronzed and smooth, and Pat's pale and mottled and blue with the veins of a very old person whose lifetime of sewing and piano playing and gardening and baking and painting and soothing and comforting and waving and hugging and sailing and golfing and praying showed in every spot and wrinkle and gnarled joint.

"I'm here," she said again. "I know I haven't been by since the last time we said goodbye, but I guess you really are going away this time. At least that is what they told me, so I came to see you one last time, Granny. Just this one last time to say goodbye and thank you for every single wonderful thing you ever did for me. I know I wasn't always the easiest person to be around, and I know I've done a lot of things I'm not very proud of, but I tell you, Granny, I think I'm growing up at last. I think I'm ready to say goodbye to the bad things in my life and I just wanted you to know I wouldn't be who I am without you. I'm sorry I couldn't tell you these things before now, and I know they say you can't hear me or understand what I am saying, but I know deep in my heart that somehow you do know, and you know how much I love you even when I didn't seem to love myself. I'll miss you, Granny. I miss you already."

She started to tell her about The Typing Room and the ad and the letter and just as she was speaking an astonishing thing happened, something that very often does happen when Death arrives to take your last walk with you. Pat opened her eyes. They were bright and clear and she turned to the child of her heart and spoke to her as rationally and honestly as any conversation they had ever had before she got sick.

"Don't be sad, Sweetie, I'm doing just fine now. I can see your grandfather is waiting for me, so I have to run. By the way, I don't like that fellow of yours one bit. He shows a decided lack of salt, if you know what I mean. You can do better, my dear. Go out and find some nice young man, someone who can share your happiness." And then she exhaled and died.

Sweetie called for the nurse and her family and the nurse took Pat's vitals and pronounced to the family that the patient has expired. In fact she said it twice and stated the time of death each time. She asked them if they wanted a sheet pulled over the face, and nodded when they declined. She made the final entry to the chart and left the room to call the physician in charge so that the official notation could be signed off and make it a legal death. The hospice worker asked if they wanted a minister, but Granny had already received the last blessings, so there was no real point, and they would arrange with their own church for the burial service. The family thanked all of the aides and nurses and workers and waited until the funeral home arrived to take away the body. Sweetie made no mention of her Grandmother's last advice. She knew it was hers alone.

The young man who came was dressed in a suit and tie and his grooming was impeccable, from neatly trimmed hair and buffed nails to the spit and polish shine on his shoes. Walter and the boys left the room, but Sweetie elected to stay to help him prepare the body for transfer from the bed to the gurney he brought with him and for the walk to the elevator and down to the van waiting at the back of the hospital. He was very gentle with her, much to Sweetie's relief, as they swathed her in a white shroud from head to toe and then draped her entire body in a dark blue wool blanket. Sweetie wanted a lock of hair, which the man helped her with by supplying a small pair of scissors and a ribbon just for such requests. When they were ready, he moved the gurney to the doorway and leaned out, giving the aide at the end of the hall a discreet wave. As if on cue, all the doors along the corridor began to close slowly and shut without making a sound. The nurses and the aides gathered together and waved goodbye, some of them quietly crying even though they knew Thanatos was a frequent caller in this wing.

~~~

"Goodbye, Pat," The Proprietress said, "Godspeed."

"So long, ol' gal, don't forget to write!" said the cranky one.

"'Till we meet again, I guess," said another.

"Goodbye," said Harry. "It was nice to meet you."

"Bye bye," said Alfonso.

And so on until all the farewells had been made.

Chapter XXIV

Jack had all the poise of a nine-year-old schoolboy on the way to his first coed dance. He looked the part, his heart on fire and his head whirling with ideas and images for the new life he hoped to share with precious Nimfa, with whom he'd spoken that morning to confirm their late afternoon lunch in the cafeteria at Madison. He spent extra time with this morning's ablutions, and wore his most well cut suit and his favorite Jerry Garcia tie which everyone complimented him on when he wore it. When he got home that morning from The Typing Room, he was too energized to sleep, still under the euphoria of spiritual salvation, so he pulled out the shoeshine kit he kept on the top shelf of his closet and polished and brushed his shoes to a gleaming finish. He took a cab because he did not want to risk tight quarters on the bus, lest his suit become creased, or his shoes stepped on. He wished he could get a quick haircut and an even closer shave at the barber shop at the corner, but it was closed until nine, and he wanted to get to his office on time to check his safe deposit box.

He opened his office and Elaine wiggled over to say good morning. "You look absolutely delicious, Jack! Are you going out for a promotion?" He did not want to speak to anyone least he burst forth with a plethora of private thoughts and personal desires, but she asked about his visit to the hospital the day before and he explained ever so politely he would have to return later to again visit his sick friend. "Oh, I see, a sick friend," she said, winking at him. "Well, aren't you the loyal one." Without doubt, this was certainly a debatable point; however, even this did little to minimize the delightful sense of anticipation he was feeling. "I have the key right here, shall we go in?" she asked when he indicated he wanted to visit his box.

When he was alone, in the cocoon of the viewing cubicle, he pulled the letter he found in The Typing Room and reread the part about "appropriate compensation." He was more than stunned when he found the box very nearly empty of the money he had received as payment for ensuring his friend Harry's demise. But it was a momentary sting, because after all he had pretty much screwed the pooch on that one. However, given the previous withdrawal of two thousand and what appeared to be missing now, he figured he still had about one hundred thousand dollars. "Clever one, that Typing Room," he mused. There was also another crème-colored envelope, but smaller this time, more of a note card than a letter.

The small card was of the same heavy paper, embossed with the initials "TTR" in a monogram style on the front. Inside was a handwritten note.

Dear Mr. Hollinger,

By now you know the price of deliverance from perdition. But we trust you will find the remaining amount acceptable with which we hope you will begin life renewed as is your mind no doubt. Please accept our thanks for a wonderful story of liberation and we hope to hear from you again, should the need arise at any time.

Sincerely,

The Typing Room

He sat back in the chair and laughed. He couldn't quite fathom feeling so good about losing over four hundred thousand dollars, and didn't even want to spend time trying to figure out how in blazes they got to the money, because he did feel changed and for the better. He looked over the contents of the box, and pulled out the Polaroids which he would shred later, and put them in his inside breast pocket, from which he produced the silver flask, newly filled. He knew an occasional sip for medicinal purposes only, of course, would do little harm in the grand scheme of things, and then he took the box with the ring and put it in his coat pocket. Two o'clock would be here before he knew it.

Meanwhile, in The Typing Room, The Proprietress and the others were putting the finishing touches on a new ad.

> *"Need Cash for a Worthy cause? No Time to go through the Usual channels? Don't Worry and don't Wait. Come One...Come All to The Typing Room! We pay good honest Money for your Story of Petition and Prayer."*

Even Harry helped on this one. It was the least he could do.

Chapter XXV

It was official. Alfonso would be moved to another hospital and placed on dialysis while he waited for a kidney, one which would probably not come in time. "If all is really fair in love and war, then I have nothing to lose," Nora thought as she went to the administrator's office to find out what could be done to keep Alfonso in Madison, under her direct care. The meeting was short and final. There was not enough money to keep the boy under the care of a practically private nurse, and though they did not say this in so many words, what was the point since he was not going to wake up, and given his age, would be under their care far longer than even the elderly patients in the East Wing. Frankly, she was told, it's a matter of what makes sense, as in dollars and cents. It wasn't that they were unfeeling, or that they wanted to condemn him to an early grave, of course not, but all the same, the use of the staff and facilities here at Madison would best be spent, in their fiscally framed opinion, on the care of a more promising patient or bottom line, one who could pay. She had until two o'clock.

Checking her bank account and finding it wanting, she called her accountant and was told, as she well knew, most of her money was tied up in long-term funds, which would all but vanish if she took the money out now. With that it would be a mere pittance to lay out at the feet of hospital management and pitiably not enough to persuade them to delay the plan to move the boy that afternoon.

After that, on her break, Nora walked over to the church where she often went to pray and where on Sundays, she lit candles for all her former patients who had died; all twelve of them. She prayed fervently and lit another, larger candle for Alfonso. She felt confident, as do all believers, that God would send her a sign and that whatever happened, all was in divine order. She did not pray for money. She knew better than that. She simply explained the problem and said thank you for an expected solution. Whatever it might be, she could not be sure, only that there would be one.

She vowed to keep her eyes and ears open to the possibilities, because she understood that oftentimes the voice of God is a whisper on the wind, or a faint delectable scent, or a line from a poem suddenly brought to mind. It comes in a dream, or a desire, or in a conversation overheard on the bus, or on line at the supermarket; or in the eyes of a newborn or in the worn face of the dying; sometimes it is a gesture of kindness or a smile from a stranger, or the blue of the sky or the pink of a rose. Sometimes it is none of these things. Sometimes it is an ad.

On the walk back, she saw it, stapled to the telephone pole at the corner near the crosswalk where she exited from the side door of the church. It had not been there before, she was sure of that, though she could have easily missed it now were she not keenly aware of her surroundings, one of the fringe benefits of a prayerful life. It was a small crisp white card, bordered in black, with neat type. It promised good, fast money for a precious cause. There was nothing rational in her decision to go to this place. It was foolish really, but she had faith, given that the cause was more precious to her than her own life. She took the card and checked her watch. She, and Alfonso, had less than three hours.

As she stood at the bus stop, a cab pulled up and the driver asked if she wanted a ride. She took this as another sign and hopped in, tipping the driver five dollars for a ten-dollar fare. She asked if he might return about one fifteen, so she could get back to the hospital quickly. He'd been a patient at Madison, he told her and had received first-rate care. He knew somehow he could not fail this woman. Her face was gleaming, and he felt perhaps she was on a special mission from the hospital. He nodded.

She climbed the stairs and walked right in without knocking. She saw the typewriter and sat down on the chair, dropping her bag on the desk. She tore open the envelope which was placed there and read the letter so carefully written:

Dear Nurse Poole,

We appreciate you are pressed for time, and understand how important it is for you to return in an expeditious manner, so we will keep our letter short and to the point. We know about Alfonso.

In exchange for a brief summary of your feelings and future plans for him, we stand prepared to supply you with sufficient capital to retain him under your care at his present location. It will be enough. No more will be needed as you will come to know in time.

The Typing Room

We do not expect another visit from you; therefore allow us this opportune moment to let you know how very appreciative we are to you in ways you cannot imagine for your compassionate and committed work at the hospital.

Please mind the quarters in the dish and the basket where you should place the pages. Please sign the last page, using the pen and not the pencil, and note the code from the bottom of the ad. We ask that you turn the lamp on before you leave. When you return, please call your bank again. The transfer of funds will be complete upon receipt of your story.

Sincerely,

The Typing Room

She wrote about her little sparrow and about how Alfonso came to be under her wing, and how with each day caring for him she felt less lonely and less vulnerable in the world, a feeling which no one would ever in their wildest imaginings suspect rested with her daily because she had perfected the veneer of invincibility and had tightly wrapped herself with the protective blanket of unqualified competence which most people admire from a distance, but disdain upon closer inspection.

She was like a rough round stone passed by frequently as ordinary, but which when struck open reveals beautiful crystals, or a spiny, misshapen desert cactus which blooms only after a flash flood, and then only for a day until wasps lay their eggs in the bloom and kill the plant. She loved him and wrote about loving him until death. He was her child now, and she was not going to let him go. Whatever this place was or by what means this money made its way to her, she did not care to know. She only saw this as a prayer answered, serene in the knowledge that the details were entirely in the hands of God and that these people, whoever they might be, were only acting at His direction.

"See, I told you so," said The Proprietress to Harry. "We are merely the paint, not the artist."

"What happens now?" asked Harry. "Will he go back?"

"Oh, yes," she said. "He will be going back very shortly, so let's all say our goodbyes quickly. We will not see him this way again." And so as they did with Pat, they all sent Alfonso off with a cheerful wave.

"I miss the patter of little feet already," Harry mused.

"So do I," said The Proprietress. "But the best is yet to come, I am sure of that."

"How do you mean?" he asked.

"Wait and see," she said.

"Why do I always feel like Ferlinghetti in this place?"

"And what exactly do you mean by that remark?"

"You know, Lawrence Ferlinghetti, 'I am perpetually awaiting a rebirth of wonder'?'" he said, thinking, "A-ha! I've finally found a reference which is beyond her."

"Yes, Harry, you are," she said sweetly, "Absolutely."

And with that Alfonso opened his eyes.

Chapter XXVI

At precisely two o'clock, Jack stepped into the cafeteria at Madison. He had brought flowers, all the while wondering if that was entirely appropriate for just a lunch date, but since it was a date, he felt comfortable with the small gesture. Most women liked flowers; he hoped Nimfa would like the colorful selection he'd picked up at the corner. He did not see her at first, but looking around he caught her looking out for him. She smiled. How vivid and beautiful her smile was to him. She had two cups in front of her, and for an instant Jack thought someone else had been sitting with her, but no, the coffee was for him. A warm welcome, as she stood to greet him.

"Hello, Jack," she said, her eyes bright and attentive.

"Hello, Nimfa," he said, sighing deeply. "I'm so glad to see you."

"Me, too," she said, "Actually, I was worried I would not be able to come because there is a lot of commotion in the hospital this afternoon."

"Oh? What happened?"

"Didn't you hear on your way in? It's a miracle. None of the doctors are able to explain it at all. I think they do not want to call it that, but that is what it is, I know."

Jack must have looked a bit confused, but curious, so she went on.

"A young patient in the West Wing, who has been in a coma for almost two years suddenly woke up!"

"Really? Exactly what happened? These are for you, by the way," he said, giving her the flowers.

"Oh, these are really lovely. How thoughtful you are."

"I hope you like them...I don't know about flowers, but some of them smell quite nice."

"Yes, these are freesia and the yellow ones are called Peruvian lilies, and the orange ones are Gerber daisies." She said as she caressed each flower.

"You know about flowers, then?"

"Yes, I love to garden. Someday I will have a home with a very large backyard and I will grow flowers and tomatoes and beans and then more flowers."

"I will get that for you," thought Jack. "I will get you whatever will keep you in my life looking at me the way you are looking at me right now."

"By the way," he said. "Would you like to eat somewhere else? There is a lovely café right down the street."

"Oh, I cannot leave. I am due back in only forty five minutes, so perhaps we should get something from the counter now."

So they went to the food-service area and took pleasure in making their selections, most of which were exactly the same, right down to the lime green Jell-O squares which wiggled on the tray as they walked back to the table. She asked him questions about his job and where he lived and wondered if he had been up the ward to see his friend, who it seems was doing rather well, though he had not reawakened. All around them, people were talking about the "miracle" in the West Wing.

"He just opened his eyes, I tell you. I couldn't believe it when I came on duty. Every specialist in the place is going to see for themselves."

"He's such a cute kid. Has he said anything yet?"

"No, I heard he hasn't made a sound, though he is completely alert, because they've tested all his other senses, and he seems to hear well, and see well and can follow all their directions."

"But he can't talk, eh? Is he breathing on his own?"

"That was the first thing they did. You know, taking the trach out. But he hasn't said a word. What's totally amazing is that he is more than awake, he is well. They must have misdiagnosed him."

"Tell me, Nimfa," said Jack, wanting to take her hand, but not wanting to be that forward so quickly. "Do you believe in miracles?"

She paused for a moment, and then she said "Yes. Yes, I do. I've seen and heard things which make me believe that sometimes God pulls back the veil just ever so slightly and gives us a small illustration of His goodness."

"You think this boy waking up is a sign, then?"

"A sign? I'm not sure. All I know is that he was very nearly dead and now suddenly he is alive. Whatever they say medically, it's a miracle. Don't you think so?"

"Me, oh, I'm inclined to believe that things are never exactly what they seem to be. I'm not a really religious guy, you see. In fact, I can't remember when I was in church last except for a funeral. Not since I was a kid, I guess," he said. "Is religion important to you? I mean, do you go to church or anything?"

"Oh, yes," she said. "Maybe you would like to come sometime?"

Jack was not unreasonably concerned that the roof might cave in on him if he did, but he thought it might be worth the risk to sit with her in a pew and sing some songs and kneel, or whatever they did in church these days and find out more about any and everything that was essential to her. "Okay. Yes, that sounds like a plan."

"Good, here is my address," she said, writing it on a little piece of paper she tore from a small notebook pulled from her pocket. "I live with my sisters and my auntie. We can all go together this Sunday if that is all right. And afterwards maybe you can stay for supper. We cook a big meal on Sundays and everyone comes over to visit."

Jack was impressed that she wanted him to meet her family so quickly, and felt possibly this was a cultural peculiarity. He fingered the small velvet box in his pocket. Perhaps if he did not pass muster with them, their romance was doomed, so he vowed to put his best foot forward and to show how serious he was, he asked her a question. "Is there something I can bring? Anything. Just tell me."

"Well," she said, almost shyly. "I noticed the other day you had a cigar sticking out of your pocket. My uncle smokes cigars, and I'm sure he would appreciate having a smoke with you after dinner. I'm afraid all of us have a tendency to shoo him out on the patio alone, do you know what I mean?"

Jack was relieved. He thought he might have to prepare a dish or something. "Of course. Yes, I'll bring a couple and have a smoke with him," he said. "And chocolates? Do your sisters and aunt like chocolates?" She nodded. "I'll bring a big box."

"It will be fun," she said. "But now I have to get back to my ward. Thank you, Jack, for lunch, and for these flowers. Please pick me up at nine-thirty?"

"I'll be there, Nimfa." He made a note of how delicate her hands were and vowed to have the ring sized at the jewelry shop down the street from his office.

And he walked her to the elevator and waited until she got in and the door closed. He turned and was in a bit of a daze when he collided with a frazzled woman hurrying down the hall, carrying a tray of food.

"I'm so sorry," he said. "May I help you there?"

"No, I'm sorry," she said picking up the dishes. "It was my fault, really."

"Please, let me help you." He looked in her eyes and remarked to himself how incredibly blue they were, like the waters of the Caribbean.

"No, it's okay, I'll get an orderly. It's just that I was in a hurry. I was late this morning to work, and now I'll be late again, I guess, to my next shift."

"Are you sure there's nothing I can do?"

"No, I'm fine," she told him, but as she walked away Jack felt there was some quiet note of anxiety which would erupt to anger if she crossed paths with anyone else.

~~~

141

He went back to his office and shredded the photos and the letter and the ad from The Typing Room and, removing the plastic bag from the machine, took it outside to the back of the building and threw it in the dumpster, just as the trash truck was coming up the alley.

Jack thought ahead to Sunday, and called his connection about the cigars. Just to be sure, he ordered an entire box. His new life was at last beginning.

"So, will he marry her, do you think?" asked Harry.

"He is a damn fool if he doesn't," answered The Proprietress.

Chapter XXVII

The eyes of a child are like the stars in the night sky, full of wonder and mystery that pose the enduring questions all philosophers and theologians have been asking and attempting to answer since the first person looked up at the sky and then noticed how small they were when compared to the vastness of space. "Why am I here? And where is here exactly?" "Am I alive?" "Where am I going?" "What will I find when I get there?'" "Am I loved?"

"Alfonso," Nora said gently when she walked into his room. Even before she arrived at his door, she was met with several nurses and aides, all joyful with the news of his veritable resurrection. When the doctors and the rest of the staff saw her coming, they parted to let her pass and one by one moved out of the room so she could be alone with the boy.

"Alfonso."

"Nora!" he cried and threw his arms open wide, begging her to pick him up out of the bed. She rushed over to him and scooped him upright, ever mindful that he had been immobile for months and months save the exercises she did for him. He was able to sit up and clung to her with all the tenacity of a young koala grabbing on to the fur of its mother's belly, lest he plunge to the ground from the high canopy of eucalyptus branches.

"Oh, my dear child," she said through her tears. "You've come back to me."

"I was here, mostly, Nora, except when I went to the other place. It was nice and there was another lady there who was nice, too. But I told her I wanted to come back and see you, so she and the other people sent me back."

"I see," she whispered, not wanting to contradict him for having what was in all probability a hallucination or a dream. "When you are all better, you can tell me more about it, but right now I want to talk with the doctors and make sure you are sound as a penny, okay?"

She was not used to this feeling of love. It was uncharted territory and she did not want to frighten or overwhelm Alfonso with her new found bliss until she was more at ease with it. Practically speaking, she still held some fear he might not be able to come home with her since all the legalities would take some time and he still needed time to rebuild his strength. But for the moment, as she held him in her arms, she was content with imagining a future conversation, asking how he might feel about coming to live with her

~~~

"Do you think you might want to come home to live with me, Alfonso?"

"Oh, yes, Nora. Can I?"

"Yes, I was thinking we might have to get a house because my apartment is kind of small."

"Can we get one with a yard?"

"Well, I think a yard would be nice."

"And could we get a dog? I'd love to have a dog."

"We'll go down to the shelter and you can pick one out..."

~~~

She had done some quick calculations and figured the newly deposited sum of two hundred and fifty thousand would more than cover a small cottage with a yard and a dog and a child, and the lawyer and the realtor who would make them possible.

"I love you, Nora," he said, yawning from a natural desire to sleep.

"I love you, too, dearie."

"I think I'm going to cry," said Harry, and noticeably the least bit sarcastically. "We'd better hope he never wonders about the lady in the nice place, I guess, huh?"

"He will have forgotten about it by the time he wakes up. For the young, to forget is oftentimes a blessing."

"But not when you're old, right?"

"No, not when one is old," said The Proprietress. "A failing mind is a sad beginning to an even sadder end."

"Will he and Nora be happy at last?"

"I think they will. I think they deserve it, don't you?"

Pleased that she seemed to value his opinion, he nodded and said nothing in case he said something idiotic and ruined the pleasure of this modest but well-earned victory.

Chapter XXVIII

Men can be deliciously solicitous until the moment comes, as it inevitably does in any relationship, wherein the woman realizes she has needs that are different than his and has the audacity to point it out. In a love affair where two equals position themselves toe to toe, both vertically and horizontally as often as possible, through whatever trials and tribulations may come, there is the possibility of a long and happy courtship and perhaps a marriage of both physical and mental halves resulting over time in a fully formed and greater whole. Sadly, this was not the case in the romance of Sweetie and Roan.

"I can't believe you just up and fuckin' quit!" bellowed Roan into his cell phone, on his way to yet another pressing meeting. "Are you crazy?"

"Stop shouting at me, Roan." said Sweetie in a composed and collected tone of voice as if speaking to someone with borderline IQ scores. "And no, I am not crazy, I quit because I am leaving for New York on Sunday. I have the plane ticket right in front of me and I am packing my bags as we speak." She had used the money she got from her visit to The Typing Room for a one-way, first-class ticket into JFK.

"What about us? Are you telling me I mean nothing to you?"

"Are you telling me that I mean 'anything' to you? Or am I just one in a series of easy lays you had before me and will probably have long after I am gone?"

"Where is this coming from? We've been together for a long time, my girl. Haven't I always put you first?"

"It's amazing to me that you actually believe that. I mean you do, don't you? You think that meeting you at your convenience for a quick fuck is putting me first. Which one of us is really in need of psychiatric help, Roan? You, the perpetrator of this sham of a relationship, or me for letting you get away with it? My God, you do lack salt."

"What's that...you're breaking up...can you hear me?"

"Nothing," she said, "It's just something my grandmother warned me about."

"Look, baby," said Roan, making a course correction in a conversation which was not going the way he wanted it to. "I know you're upset about your grandmother. She was a wonderful old gal and I know how much you loved her. Maybe you need to take some time and think about this before you make another mistake. I mean, quitting your job? What are you going to do for money when you get to New York? It's a helluva lot more expensive to live there than this town, I promise you. And it's not like secretaries make enough to pay much more than the rent."

"I have what I need," she said. "And I'll be fine. I'm going back to school to see what I can make of my life. I want to start from scratch and find out what makes me happy, Roan. I don't want to grow old having my happiness depend on someone as distracted as you are by their own ambitions and parochial attitudes about marriage. You're married! You're married, for Christ's sake. You have a wife and children and you will never, ever do anything to change that, and I have been a sad and stupid, blind fool to think you ever would." She was crying now, the catharsis of truth opening up the floodgates of her heart. She had so much more to say, but thought better of wasting her words on a deaf man. "Pearls before swine!" Granny Pat would have said.

Roan was quiet for a minute, because somewhere in his reptile brain, there was a glimmer of truth to what she said, but not one which he wanted to have interfere with his perfectly patterned life. "So what you're telling me is that it's over." It was a statement rather than a question.

"Yes, it's over."

His tone was rigid and spiteful and brusque. "Okay then. If that's what you want. Will you call me when you get there? I mean, I do want to know how to reach you in case I'm in town there, you know, maybe we can meet for a drink?"

"Sure, Roan, I'll call you when I get there," she said and quietly hung up the phone, having no intention whatsoever of giving him a way to track her or ever interfere with her life again. As far as she was concerned, he was dead to her and she did not want to be haunted by the ghost of her poor choices or otherwise be reminded of days spent wondering if they would see each other or what outfit to wear that might please him or what last-minute worry she might have of getting discovered by a fellow employee, or his wife. She wanted to forget all about him and the last seven years.

"So, she'll stay in Pat's apartment?" asked Harry.

"Yes, it's hers now, along with a generous inheritance," said The Proprietress.

"The Big Apple," Harry said. Just the sound of it evokes a stir in one's emotions. "New York, the best and brightest city in the world. How I wish I had gone there before...well, before all this."

"Why didn't you?"

"I guess I figured there would always be time."

"Time to do the things you now know you never will."

"Yeah, I suppose it's true, if only I'd known then what I know now."

"I would not focus on that too long, Harry. It can only make you unhappy now. Better to take a measure of delight in the things you did do and not the things you did not."

"Okay, then," said Harry. "Who's next?"

"I think a trip to Atlantis is in order," said The Proprietress.

Chapter XXIX

"Dearest Petunia,

I got your letter this morning. I'm so happy about the baby. I can't wait to see you and my girls, so I have sent you some money from my first paycheck so you can begin to save to come out and join me. I know it is not much, but I will send more each week until you all are able to come here. I have sent a letter to the boys also, and a little money for them and your mother. I miss you, Sweetheart. Kiss the girls for me.

Your loving husband,

Rusty Storm."

Corrine carried the letter in the pocket of her gray smock as she clocked in late again for her second shift of the day. She'd already been warned, so it was a sure bet her supervisor, Mr. Jacobs, would want to have a talk with her again today. It would not be so bad except he always wanted to have these talks in his office with the door shut so no one could hear him make indirect crude suggestions to her about how, in spite of her obvious disregard for hospital protocol, she might keep the job he had a feeling she would do almost anything to keep.

"I see by the timecards that you've been late almost every shift, Corrine. Is there something wrong at home? Are you having personal problems which keep you from being at work on time? You know that here at Madison we take special pride in giving the very best care to our patients and that includes everything from the finest medical care to the outstanding janitorial maintenance, and that in between is the first-rate food service we provide the patients and the staff." She had heard this same diatribe before, as if Madison would be rocked to its very foundation by one mistimed meal. And yet he continued as if she had not heard it before.

"And to that goal, it is up to each and every member of my team to do their part. You would not want Miguel to be late, would you? Or Winnie? Or perhaps you think we can do without Oscar?"

"No, sir," she said. Miguel was the chief cook. Mr. Jacobs could drop dead from a coronary, but nothing would get prepared in this kitchen without Miguel. They referred to him as the CFO, – Chief Fridge Officer. And Winnie was in charge of the paperwork for what tray of food went to which patient. She kept the low-sodium meals from going to the patients who really needed food rich in glucose, and vice versa. And Oscar made sure that when the dishes were returned, they were scrubbed and cleaned to a "see yourself" shine ready for the next round of service. No, she did not want to let them down, it was Mr. Jacobs she wished would somehow stick his hand in the garbage disposal and be sucked in whole, inch by inch, never to be heard from again, after the screaming subsided, naturally.

"So we won't have any more of this, because the next time you are late, I'm afraid I will have to put you on disciplinary leave until whatever is preventing you from keeping up with the team has been dealt with? Is that clear, Corrine?"

"Yes, sir," she said without looking into the dull wateriness of his pale gray eyes. "It's clear."

"Excellent," he said, putting his arm around her shoulder. She felt her morning sickness coming back in a strong wave and wondered how much leave he might give her if she threw up all over his shoes.

"Of course, if you should ever feel the need for some 'overtime,' Corrine, I'm sure I could use help in the office here. Sorting paperwork, you know, that type of thing? Perhaps some dictation? A man in my position can always use a little extra help now and again. I'm sure you understand, hmmm?"

She was just about to answer when her small embryo decided to swim the backstroke in its self-contained pond of warm salty broth. Poor Mr. Jacobs; those cheap shoes and his awful tie all covered up in a layer of yellow and white froth, the scent of bile mixing with his ghastly cologne. Corrine must have sounded like she was dying with each successive wretch because there was a knock at the door, and getting no answer, Winnie stepped in thinking there might be some kind of emergency. She paused for a moment and wished she'd had a camera with which to capture the look on her boss's face. "If only I had been so clever," she thought. "Maybe that'll teach the old goat!" She rushed to help Corrine to the bathroom down the hall while Mr. Jacobs fled to the adjacent men's room.

Once inside the tiled haven, she waited patiently while Corrine finished her mission. She helped her to the sink and gave her a handful of paper towels to wipe her face and the front of her smock. "Here, give me that. I'll toss it in one of the laundry baskets. We can get another one from the supply closet."

Corrine was crying softly, out of embarrassment and the sinking awareness that she would probably get fired. "There, there, honey, don't you go and worry nothin' about this. That old fart deserved every bit of upset you hurled at him," she said laughing, and wiping Corrine's tears. "Lord, thank you for sending me a witness to that evil little man's torment. 'Bout time he got some of his own, I say. When is the baby due, honey?"

"December. Christmas, I think. I don't know yet exactly because I haven't been able to see the doctor."

"Lord, child, all these doctors here and you haven't seen one about your condition. You stay right here. I'm going to call for one of the nurses in North Wing. You know that here at Madison 'we take special pride in giving the very best care.'" she said as they both suppressed a laugh. "Anyway, they'll get you in right quick to see someone. Shall I call your husband to come get you? Best if you go home to rest after you get your checkup."

"Not unless you want to call long distance," she sighed. "He's gone again, Winnie. Gone to Florida of all places. But he did write to me and the girls," she said, giving Winnie the letter.

Winnie read it and knew from everything Corrine had ever said about her life that she wildly loved her husband, even though he did always seemed to be running off. "Well, at least he's workin'. Can't say bad things 'bout a man who works to support his wife and children," she said. "When do you plan on joining him?"

"I don't know. If I lose my job, I'm worried I might not get there before the baby comes. Then what will I do? No job, two little girls and a baby? I don't know."

"Oh, I think Mr. Jacobs will leave you alone for the moment. He doesn't know you're pregnant, does he?"

"No, I haven't told anybody."

"Good, keep it that way. No use giving him more excuses to pressure you, but you will have to get here on time from now on. Your sickness should stop in the next couple of weeks. Just like that; course you know, you've got four." Corrine knew that Winnie had four also, older than hers, all boys. Their father was in the army and all four children were either in the military or ROTC, preparing for their time in the service.

"I was never this sick before," said Corrine, and then became suddenly concerned. "You don't think anything is wrong, do you? Maybe all this stress is bad for the baby?"

"Now, don't go gettin' all worked up again. I'm sure everything is just fine. You stay here and calm yourself. I'll tell Mr. 'J' that you're going home sick. There's nothing he can do about it, especially if you get a note, which you should do for your own sake. Officially, until you get a blood test, you don't know if you're pregnant so it won't make no difference which kind of doctor you see. I'll just be a minute." And then she left.

Corrine sank down against the wall and sat on the floor, which to the cleaning crew's credit was spotless. She was so tired. If only she could just lie down and sink into the coolness of the floor, or blend into the smoothness of the wall. She read Rusty's letter and wondered how she got to be in such a troubled situation, but saw no use in dwelling on it. He had sent her money. That was good. He was happy about the baby. That was good, too. The girls were happy, or at least Aimee was, and in spite of her current tummy troubles, she was in good health. "Good Oklahoma stock is what you're from, girl, so stop your whining." This was her mother's considerate way of comforting her whenever things went wrong, which unfortunately seemed to be more and more often, especially since Rusty left. "Maybe," she thought, "I should just write to Rusty and have him come back and take care of Mr. Jacobs." But she knew she would never tell her husband, because he would just kill the bastard and that would only cause another problem. Besides, much like her own mother, Corrine had a mean right cross and could easily take him down with one punch if things ever got beyond the suggestion phase.

Winnie returned in less than five minutes. "Well, you look a little better. Get up, child and I'll walk you upstairs to see Dr. Sanchez. She's one of the young ones, but you'll feel comfortable with her, I'm guessing. Oh, I'm not sure you know about this yet," she said as they went up in the elevator. "But did you hear about the boy in West Wing?"

"No, not really. What's up?"

"Like Lazarus, I tell you. Praise God, is what I say. He was in a coma and definitely on his way out, if you get my meaning. And, Lord, he's not only up, he's well! So you see child, miracles happen all the time; you just got to know where to look."

Dr. Sanchez was very kind. She sent her down to the lab for a blood test and wrote her a note, leaving out the possibility of a pregnancy, and told her to go home. She told Corrine she was about eight weeks along and unless the blood test showed anything unusual, she was to begin taking vitamins and to try and get more rest.

Corrine thought things were beginning to look up until she got behind the wheel of her clunker. It would not start. Try as it might, the engine was just too old and worn out to crank even once. All that was left for it was a trip to the junkyard. "Oh, God, Rusty! Will we ever get to that blue water? Will I even be able to pick up the girls today from school?" She was exasperated and tired and hungry and sad, and no measure of strapping genetics was going to help her more practical problems. So she began to walk home. No use wasting bus fare, when what she really needed was some food. It would be a long walk, but she felt she could use the fresh air and the exercise was probably okay, as long as she didn't push it and got something to eat along the way. Actually, it would be the first afternoon in a very long time she would have time to herself to just walk and window shop and take in the world instead of always looking down on the ground like an ant.

About thirty minutes into her travels, she found "Rocky's -- Home of the Splendid Burger," a little hamburger stand, next door to the fire station. The grilling meat and onions, far from making her queasy, ramped up her appetite and she ordered a double chili cheeseburger with everything and onion rings fried to a deep delectable golden brown. A large Coke brought the total to four dollars and eighty six cents. Exactly what she had in her purse and no more. "Well," she thought, trying to justify what was in her reality a huge splurge, "At least I won't have to eat tonight, and there is that package of chicken

drumsticks in the freezer. I can make those for the girls."
She took her tray and sat at one of the small tables at the
back of the stand. There was a pleasant breeze blowing
and the sun was still bright in the sky. She figured she had
at least two hours before she would have to pick up the
girls from the after-school program.

She took out the letter from Rusty and read it again. *"I
will send more each week until you all are able to come
here."*

For the heck of it, she took out a pen from her purse
and tried to figure out exactly how long it would take
before she had enough money to make a journey cross
country to join her husband. She was not at all surprised
that the baby she was carrying in her womb would be
nearly six months old before she would be able to have
enough to buy another car, less if she and the girls took the
Greyhound, and took only their clothes. Though she loved
her husband to distraction, he absolutely had little in the
way of a clue as to how much things cost. But, like Winnie
said, he was working and that was something.

She finished her meal, licking each and every finger,
and chewing up all the ice in the white Styrofoam cup. And
for a moment Corrine was struck by how, in spite of all her
woes, life was really not too bad. The sun was shining and
she had just had a meal no king could boast was better, she
had four great kids, and a husband who was mad for her,
slaving away on some hot, steamy highway, bare-chested
and glistening from the salt water in the nearby ocean. She
smiled and waved at the cook behind the counter as she
walked to the end of the street and turned the corner. She
was a little surprised when she came upon the park, which

was just across the street from The Typing Room. She had never approached it from this street before. She'd always driven and taken a less circuitous route to and from the hospital, but the fact of having time to meander was more than she could resist, so she had walked through neighborhoods which would otherwise have gone undiscovered.

She sat on a bench looking at the building. She'd never noticed how stately it was, or how foreboding. The only window which had no curtain was the one in the front on the top floor. The one which housed The Typing Room. No one in the time she sat and watched ever came in or out of the building. She had never wondered too much about the mechanics of who ran this place, or why, or how the money got to her, or what they did with the letters she had typed there, or how they decided how much it was worth. She would never tell anyone about the ad she found that day, or about going there two times. It was as if the place didn't exist except when she went there. Maybe that was the key. Maybe this place was born out of her unhappiness and that it only appeared when she needed it to. A phantom place. One that moved in and out of this universe as if responding to her mood and her circumstances, and yet she knew others visited too. What was their influence? Were their desires as great as hers or their situation as hopeless?

"That's crazy," she admonished herself. And yet she was curious. She still had the ad folded and hidden deep in the folds of her wallet. "What would happen," she thought, "if I went there now?" Wouldn't it be funny if she walked up the four flights and found the room completely empty, or if she ran into someone else who was paying a visit there coming out? What would they say to each other? Would they look into each other's eyes only to see reflections of themselves, and then turn quickly to avoid saying hello? Or what if the person who receives the letters was there making a pickup? Would it be some wizened, withered, wealthy old crone in need of the opportunity to do good works before death forced the final confrontation at the judgment seat? Or some young punk, with an inheritance, in a creative writing class just looking for a way to cheat by turning in the stories as weekly assignments under his own signature?

Before she realized it she pulled the ad out and was more than flabbergasted.

> *"Feeling Overburdened? Need to Escape? Distant shores calling? Come One...Come All to The Typing Room! We pay good, honest Money for your Story of Fight and Flight."*

Chapter XXX

In the world before The Typing Room, The Proprietress had prided herself on being an exceedingly level-headed woman, not given to flights of fancy or wild imaginings, though there was the occasional outburst of anger, but only if deeply provoked. Hers was always the practical and safe approach, the one which made sense. She smoked for a time because it was fashionable, but then gave it up when medical science contended it was dangerous; she did not drink hard liquor, but did enjoy an occasional glass of wine or a good margarita. She watched her weight and her job required her to be physically fit so that she might keep up with the children whom she had charge over.

She would go every two weeks to have her hair cut and styled, and had it dyed a warm honey brown until, with advancing age, she allowed it to go soft and silvery grey, feeling it might afford her a better reception when flashing her senior citizen discount card to look at least as old as she was. But when she was in her prime, she took her time in the evenings about her personal grooming. She never went to bed without a freshly scrubbed face and a touch of night cream. She loved to wear Shalimar and Chanel #5. Her shoes were always shined and her garments fresh from the laundry or the dry cleaners. She would have her nails professionally done but did her own pedicures, because she felt anything else was a bit too personal, besides she thought her feet were less than attractive. She and her husband would go out to the nightclubs and listen to the big bands play and they would dance and laugh and kiss under the shimmering lights of the ballroom floor. If only she could remember.

She had four children, all decent, hardworking, caring human beings any mother could be proud of. And she had five grandchildren, each one finding their place in the world, some with children of their own. But by the time her first great-grandchild had come to be born, she was already at the point of minimal thought and speech. They presented a new baby boy to her, but she could only smile and think to herself, "What a cute baby. I wonder whose it is?"

The only thing that mattered was what was happening at the moment it occurred. With no point of reference, every moment was as the first, and so she existed suspended in a kind of time warp, with no future and no past. It was a hell not unlike being a prisoner of war. Every day was the same torturous existence and no one could blame you if you gave up hope.

She was fed and bathed and clothed regularly. She was aware of the aides she liked and the ones who were less than happy with the work, but by and large, she was well cared for by a group of women and some men who probably regarded her in the same respectful light as their own grandmothers or aged aunties. Her family visited often and they spent time getting to know the staff, but after a while even they had to get on with their lives and she did not really know if they were there or not. She wasn't. She was in The Typing Room. The dream was her first clue that she hadn't really lost anything in spite of the medical propaganda that said her brain cells were being choked into oblivion by some tenacious sticky matter the nature of which no one could explain, or that she had endured multiple microscopic strokes and that the diminishing number of cells would eventually prevent her from swallowing or breathing, leading to a slow and grievous death, eaten alive from within, and that she was in fact disappearing. But she hadn't. At least not yet.

"Harry," said The Proprietress. "We need to talk."

Men, no matter where they are or how old, do not like the sound of that phrase, mainly because they are action-oriented and not generally high-verbal. Too much talking was a sure sign that they were in trouble, but give them a wrench or a hammer and a "honey-do" list and they were happy little campers.

"Somehow," Harry thought, "this can't be good."

"Now, now," she said. "I know what you are thinking. Please give me your attention because this concerns you in the most personal way."

"What is it then?"

"I'm leaving."

"Oh?"

"Is that all you have to say? 'Oh?'"

"Well, what I mean is what do you mean exactly by 'leaving?'"

"Honestly, you can be the most obtuse man. How did you pass the medical boards?"

"Now see here, I don't think it's necessary to insult me. Seems to me I've earned a little respect around here.

Haven't I been helpful, haven't I done my share to keep things running?"

"Yes, yes, you have," she said, not wanting to upset him, especially now. "Most helpful, for a man."

"See, there you go again. And what's all this about leaving? Where exactly do you think you're going?"

"I should think that was obvious," she said. "I'm going to heaven."

"The hell you say?" He found it fun to tease her, and yet he had the feeling she really meant what she said and that made him sad. Very sad indeed.

"Fine, then, I suppose there is no point in beating around the bush. I'm dying. Soon in fact, and I want you, Harry, to take over for me when I go."

Harry said nothing. He was still thinking about the part about going to heaven, wondering still if he would ever get the chance to go.

"I do believe you are going deaf. I hope not, because it will not do, you know, a deaf Proprietor." Harry said nothing.

"Well, will you or will you not?"

"What, I'm sorry, will I or won't I what?"

"Become The Proprietor and take charge of The Typing Room for me after I've gone? Will you, Harry?"

He thought for a long time. It was an enormous responsibility. And more to the point, it meant he was going to be here for a long time. He could see that now. Every time he returned to the world, it was grim. He was still hooked up to every type of life-support device, and the staff seemed very determined to keep his physical body alive. So that being the case, Harry saw this as a chance to run The Typing Room the way he felt it should be with a few updates. A laptop for one, and a gel writer pen, and a more comfortable desk chair, maybe one of those cool Eames models.

Yes," he said finally. "I will be glad to."

"Good, I knew I could count on you. Though I must admit, I wasn't sure at first. Frankly, you were a bit of a nuisance when you came, but I saw great potential. And you have proven yourself to be an entertaining companion of sorts and that has made getting to know what caliber of man you are easier and more pleasant."

"So I have met with some approval then?"

"Well, as far as I am concerned, but we still have to vote on it."

"Majority rules, I guess, huh?"

"Of course, but naturally they will respect my opinion."

"Naturally," said Harry. Maybe change the carpet to something a bit more mid-century, and add a refrigerator in case someone wanted a cold drink.

"Oh, and there's one more thing."

"What is that?"

"I want you to write a letter for me to my family."

"Okay, if that is what you wish."

"And Harry?"

"Yes?"

"If you change one thing, one tiny infinitesimal thing about that room, I will leave the comfort of heavenly hosts and take up residence in a less hospitable place just so I can come back and torment you like the Harpies, do you understand me?"

"Yes, I understand."

"Do you promise?"

"Yes, I promise."

"Do you swear?"

"I swear."

"And you'll write the letter for me?"

"Oh, yes, the letter...sure."

"Thank you, Harry," said The Proprietress. "You've made me very happy."

And with that Harry settled back and was content. "Best to leave things as they are, I suppose," he thought, because whenever a man has made a woman happy, he's accomplished something quite extraordinary.

Chapter XXXI

"Mama, are we there yet?" asked Aimee, while Doris just rolled her eyes.

"Almost, baby," replied Corrine as she drove their new pickup truck along Route 66. They passed through Tucumcari that Sunday morning, so the border of Oklahoma would be coming up quickly. "Look for the sign, girls, we'll be at your Grandma's before supper."

They would spend a couple of days with her mother. Any more would be like the old saying about guests who stay too long stink after three days. So she would pick up the boys and all of them would continue the trip to Florida where Rusty was waiting. "Are you sure you want to take the boys now?" asked her mother, not without selfish motives since they were the only field hands she had who spoke English.

"Yes, Mama, I'm sure. Rusty is expecting us at the end of the week."

"So, you won a prize, eh?"

"Yes, Mama. A new truck, can you believe it?"

"Well, frankly, no, can't say as I do, but it's better than believing you stole it, I reckon."

"I love you too, Mama." Corrine said with a soft sigh. "See you in a few days." And she hung up the phone. She had written a letter to Rusty telling him the good news. In a way she was not lying, any more than telling her story that last afternoon to The Typing Room was the closeout sale of her soul, and yet the good which had come of her three visits kept her family from becoming a welfare statistic, or a homeless problem for someone else to politicize or ostracize, depending on your point of view about such things.

After her visit, she walked the rest of the way home. She was not anticipatory in the least, but when she and the girls entered the apartment, and she found the crème-colored envelope there, she began to cry. The amount was far more generous than she ever expected. At last she could leave this town and take her daughters and sons to be with their father, and she could once again rest easy with Rusty snuggled up against her, like two spoons, at night, in the sultry breezes of a nearby ocean and they could be a family once again.

She called in the next day and quit. She noticed a hint of relief in Mr. Jacobs' voice, as he accepted her resignation and wished her luck. He did not ask her where she was going because he did not care. She wanted to call and say goodbye to Winnie and Miguel and Oscar, but did not wish to answer any questions. The Typing Room was her secret. If they were ever invited there, then that was their business just as it had been hers. She would send them a postcard when she got to Florida and they would understand and be happy for her.

The money she had left over after she left the dealership was best kept a secret also, at least for a while until the time was right to tell her husband about how a strange little room had saved them.

Chapter XXXII

Three months had passed since the woman died. The boxes of personal effects which the aides had lovingly packed for the family sat in the corner of the den in the home of her youngest daughter, untouched until now.

The funeral had been solemn and dignified, but not without the element of surprise, since there was another burial down the hill that same day and that family had arranged for a full Mariachi band to play. It was perfect, and the woman's family knew their mother would have gotten a kick out of it. The limo ride was long, but gave them time to further reminisce about a woman who would have a life-long influence on three generations. Although they thought the driver might find it odd, they asked if he would not mind pulling over at a local liquor store so they could buy another bottle of champagne with which to toast. The driver understood and obliged them.

The black marble headstone read "Adored by All," straightforward and elegant with two roses flanking her name and year of birth and death. Her husband's had been alone on the hill for nearly thirty years. It was nice to have some company after all this time.

Later that afternoon, they ate an extended meal together prepared by close friends who stood by to pay their respects. Most of the woman's friends were either dead themselves or had lost contact with the family in the many years since Alzheimer's took her away, slowly and insidiously at first, but then deliberately and quickly, so it had not been a large group.

The first box was full of clothing items, all of which would be donated or tossed depending on their condition. In the second box were photographs and cards which would be returned to the family member who originally brought them, along with silk flowers and a music box and stuffed animals which had adorned her bedside. Not very much at all, really. Not a whole lifetime's worth of stuff.

The third box was empty except for a single thick file folder and a letter in a crème-colored envelope. It was addressed simply *"Family."* The daughter was a bit annoyed that the aides or nurses had not pointed it out sooner, or even that she had not opened the boxes sooner. This was something which might have been purposeful at the rosary or at the funeral.

Inside the folder were typed pages of the same heavy and expensive paper stock. They were stories, or what might be more accurately called confessions. There was one about a hardworking woman whose beloved husband had run off with the promise of finding work elsewhere, but who had left her with two young children and one on the way. There was another from a meek little man who had apparently murdered someone but then felt sorry about it, especially since the person didn't die after all, but was now in a deep, deep coma. And then a story about a staid older woman, a nurse, who was pleading for the life of a young patient who was very near death. In it she lamented having never had a child, but begged for the life of this young boy in her care, as if he were her own. And one about a sweet young woman who had been in a torturous love affair with a much married and self-absorbed man. There were several others as well, too many to read in one sitting. Being the youngest, she supposed this collection were stories her mother had written before she became ill, but was surprised she did not know anything about them, and decided she would later ask her brothers and sisters. And then the letter.

My Dear Family,

I have asked a friend to write this letter to you which you will not be able to read until I have completed my journey home. By now the funeral festivities are long over with. I hope you did not mourn me, but rather celebrated my life with the same level of enthusiasm with which I lived.

The last ten years have been thorny for you, I know. My illness was really our illness. We shared it right down to the very last. The years you all spent taking care of me and watching over me, wondering if by some miracle I would get better, took their toll on you, but I want you to know from the very bottom of my heart how grateful I am to have had such wonderful children and grandchildren and yes, even great-grandchildren! I was truly blessed.

This admission might come as a surprise to you since I was not the most effusive and overly affectionate mother one might have hoped for. But they say still waters do run deep, and I just was not the type to be that extroverted. Funny, but I was much more comfortable saying "I love you" out loud after I got sick. Perhaps because I knew I might not be able to tell you at the end, but I want you to know how I felt, so it wasn't just because I was losing my mind. Ha ha!

Please talk about me often. I am sure I will be able, from my vantage point, to continue watching over you. Please remember all the things I taught you. To be kind, to think things out before you make a move, to favor the practical path, but not neglect any reasonable amount of fun along the way. Life can be very dull if one plays it too safe. Again, another surprise...

I have been many places and seen many things in the world, but I always knew I had my family to come home to, a special respite where I would be loved and respected and where I could always find a welcoming smile and a tender kiss. Give that same gift to each other and think of me.

Your father, aunts and uncles and cousins send their love. They were all waiting for me when I arrived, as was "Buba." I will never forget what a fuss I made when you brought her home that day from the pound, only to have her as my constant companion after your father passed away.

So don't worry about me. I am not alone and it is wonderful here. More wonderful than I could ever put into words.

Love Always,

Mom

Epilogue

The little ad was most extraordinary in its placement and in its timing. There was an address in fine print and some numbers.

> *"Confused? Is Time running out? Contemplating your next Move? Come One ... Come All to The Typing Room! We pay good, honest Money for your Story of Fear and Fraud."*

It's not like he went looking for a way in or out of this mess, but why not, maybe this place could help. He'd tried everything else. Who knew a little white collar crime like insider trading would be taken so seriously? After all, isn't a good tip meant to be shared between friends? So, he would go there that very afternoon. Not being familiar with that part of town, he entered the address into MapQuest.

"Do they always show up?" asked The Newcomer.

"Oh, yes," said The Proprietor, "it never fails."

"But what if they don't?"

"I just told you, they always come. Always."

"And then what will happen?"

"And then I will be here to receive the story, and share it with all of us," he said. "Now be patient while I write his welcome letter."

Thank you for reading.
Please review this book. Reviews help others find
Absolutely Amazing eBooks and inspire us to keep
providing these marvelous tales.

If you would like to be put on our email list to receive
updates on new releases, contests, and promotions, please
go to AbsolutelyAmazingEbooks.com and sign up.

About the Author

Monica De Vargas, in her debut novel, *The Typing Room*, explores an entirely different approach to the world of Alzheimer's patients and the nearly 16-million family caregivers in the United States whose lives are profoundly affected by this disease. "I call it 'A Comedy of Alzheimer's' in a completely respectful way, because the situations I create in the novel – some dramatic, some comical, many magical – were inspired by my mother's own gift for story-telling, sense of humor and dignity as she progressed down this painful path."

In this work of literary fiction, Monica writes from the point of view that asks the questions, "What if?" and "Why not?" spurred on by a dream she had six months after her mother's death from a nearly 12 year battle with the illness. "It unveiled itself daily, chapter by chapter, as if I were simply putting down on paper a story already written on my heart."

Monica has worked for some of the largest ad agencies in Los Angeles as a self-described "Office Mom." After a thirty-year career, she and her husband relocated from Venice Beach to a farm in rural Oklahoma. They now live in Tulsa, with their three canine companions.

The New Atlantian Library

NewAtlantianLibrary.com

or AbsolutelyAmazingeBooks.com

or AA-eBooks.com

.

www.ingramcontent.com/pod-product-compliance
Lightning Source LLC
Chambersburg PA
CBHW050404030726
47503CB00006B/2008